Married to the Enemy

A Kidnapped Groom Book

by Patricia Bates

Book Cover by Romancing the Cover

ISBN: 978-1-990536-22-9

DEDICATION

To those who have ever wanted to escape to a time and place far away from the concrete jungle where love is the ultimate prize.

AUTHOR'S NOTE

Married to the Enemy is written using the British spelling. This means some words may appear to be spelled incorrectly, this is not the case.

Thank you for reading.

Lady Patricia Bates

Chapter One

1304

Scotland

Light flickered and danced across the floor from the lamps hanging on the wall. The low buzz of voices in the room drowned out the silence as Meredith stoked the fires. She inhaled, her stomach rumbling at the aroma as fresh bread filled her nose.

A door slammed, the bang echoing along the corridors. Muffled voices darkened with rage and leased violence drifted from the end of the corridor. Meredith paused, her hand hovering over the hot loaf. Her father was in a mood - though the why escaped her.

Scuffled footsteps filled the room, and Meredith twisted around to face the door.

A young servant lass hovered in the doorway, her face ashen, eyes wide. "My lady," she met Meredith's gaze in passing, the terror in the girl's eyes pierced Meredith's composure. "Chieftain Fraser has a guest. I dared not linger, nor eavesdrop, but could not help but hear them discussing yer marriage."

Her stomach dropped at the quiver in the young woman's voice. Who could have ensured such a reaction? Her words shoved the thought aside and Meredith blanched. Marriage? Who in the name of God would dare to – "My marriage?" Meredith wiped her hands on the folded length of fabric. "There has been no–"

"Beg yer pardon, but it is themselves we can hear." She gestured over her shoulder, the volume increasing, though the words remained obscure. "There is a demand for yer hand in exchange for an alliance. In truth, I would rather be cast down to hell than marry him."

"'Tis not for us to decide, Abigail." Meredith sucked in a breath and glanced around. The usual jovial banter of the other women had faded into hushed whispers and cloying fear. "I hear them. Come, there is still bread to be pulled from the oven. I will go to Papa and see what can be done."

Skirts in hand, Meredith strode down the corridor, her heart pounding with each step. The fury in the men's voices like a swarm of hornets. She swallowed around the growing lump in her throat. Meredith approached the door, her hands shaking. Something was amiss.

"There will be peace, old man, on my terms." The harsh timber of a male voice spread through the chill clinging to the air.

"Peace, ye say. Ye want me to give ye my daughter, so ye will leave my clan alone?" Her father's voice dripped venom. "As if ye have a right to lay claim."

Like a hand wiping away the mist covering a looking glass, his words painted a picture too horrid to consider. She stumbled, her stomach dropping to her feet. What business did a Sinclair have within the walls of her home? Her father would never have sent for him. Nay, none of the Frazers had any use for the Sinclairs. Her clan was far removed from the likes of them.

"Ye ferget, Matheus, ye have no options left. The MacGhreghere has no use fer ye. Hell, at the moment he worries more fer that bitch of a wife than he does over the state of the Highlands or anyone else. Who else will agree to side with ye against the enemy? Ye standalone with nary an ally at yer backs."

"There are always options." Clatter from within the room swirled out the cracked door. Meredith pressed against the cold stone wall, a hard knot forming in her stomach. I wouldna saddle my daughter with the likes of ye fer all the gold in the Highlands. A man's temperament can be learned by looking at his horse. Ye dona deserve the animal ye have. My daughter is too good for the likes of ye.

"My son, Acair, will marry her. Our clans will join. I leave the date to ye, but I think we both agree. Ye are out of options, old man."

"I am never out of options. Get yerself out of my sight." Clipped and filled with leashed violence, Matheus's voice flooded into the corridor.

Her blood slowed through her veins. The fool actually believed he could sway her father into agreeing to such an affront? Did he have no sense?

"I will see Meredith wed to my son." The thud of footsteps approached Meredith's hiding spot, and she shuffled deeper into the shadows. "With or without yer approval. Mark my words, Matheus. Meredith will belong to my son before the end of the year or yer clan will pay for yer pride."

The door slammed into the wall. Meredith jumped, her breath catching in her throat. Heavy footfalls preceded the imposing figure of the Sinclair Chieftain as he strode into the corridor. Caelan's head brushed against the low beams of the corridor. Thick furs hung from wide shoulders to sweep the ground. Her stomach dropped and Meredith shuffled back a few steps.

He paused and turned, his narrowed gaze sweeping the room behind him. Thunder echoed within her ears when his gaze paused on her hiding spot. Good lord, surely he had not seen her. If there was a god above, he wouldna noticed her in the shadows. With a half smirk curling his lips, he turned and strode away from her hiding spot.

A fine tremble raced along her nerves. Meredith swallowed against the rising bitterness burning her throat.

The devil slithered from her home.

She sucked in a deep breath and scurried from her hiding spot. After the door closed beneath her touch, she faced her father. He sat beside the roaring fire, his hands wrapped around a cup in a white knuckle grip.. A harsh tremble gripped his hunched shoulders. He shifted, half turning to face her before facing the fire.

Meredith straightened her shoulders and walked over to kneel beside him. She reached out and grabbed one hand. Beneath her palm his skin was cold, frail almost and tears burned her eyes.

"Papa?"

"It pains me to say, my beloved daughter," Matheus faced her, his eyes drowning in tears. "But the cur is right. It is a dire situation we are in. One I prayed would not come to pass. At least until another option had presented itself."

"What do ye mean? Our allies surely have not–"

"'Tis not our allies, which is the concern, Meredith. It is the actions of others within the clan which have put us at risk. We standalone amid the turmoil, save for those who are of English persuasion. I will not see ye wed to an Englishman, Meredith. The shame would send me to an early grave."

"Papa, surely you don't mean–" Meredith's voice cracked, and she clutched his arm. It was too horrid to consider. To put any faith in.

"In truth, Sinclair is the best offer either of us may receive for yer hand. Yer marriage would put our clan back in power."

"Sinclair will not see our people to power, Papa. Nay, he will see us to ruin. The man has no desire for anything but himself."

"The elder of–"

"The son is no better than his sire." Meredith sat back. God would not permit such a demon to take over. Their people would never survive it.

"I will delay as long as I am able, Meredith. We both know in the end we need a powerful ally. Sinclair is strong."

"So is an ox."

"His men are skilled in war."

Ice closed around her heart, and she stared at her father. From the way he spoke, no words could sway him. He had made up his mind on the matter. She would be wed to Sinclair's bastard and there was naught she could say. Meredith shook her head. "It is our end to your court, Papa. Sinclair is aligned with Edward and his men. How is marrying a man with loyalties to England going to aid us?"

"Sinclair is powerful and ruthless enough to ensure our people will retain their standing–"

Her eyes burning, Meredith sucked in a shallow breath. She would not beg for crumbs from the devil himself. Sinclair was not a man worthy of anything but a sword to his neck. "He will destroy us, Papa."

"If we do nothing, our fate will be the same as the Grahams."

Meredith frowned. The Graham name had faded away with the death of the old chieftain the spring before. Once the clan members had become MacGreghere's, sworn to Callum and his wife Elizabeth, the clan flourished. Stronger than ever. "The Grahams are not slaves to the MacGregheres, Papa. They hold their lands, plant their crops."

"And none wear their clan name. Instead, they are MacGreghere's."

"By choice, ye know as well as I one of our men wed a Graham this past fall."

"Our people's future will be secure only when ye are wed and our alliance is secured."

"Nay, Sinclair will see those who are strong destroyed and make sport of the weak. Ye know this, Papa. I beg ye, find another way." Lurching to her feet, Meredith paced the confines of the room. What was being proposed was too horrid to contemplate. To know he would bind her to–nay, it was not possible.

"I know of no other way."

Meredith stared at her father. Her heart thundered beneath her ribs. "I refuse, Papa. I will never marry him." She tucked both hands into the depths of her brat to hide the trembling. "If ye desire the union, ye marry the bastard." Her voice cracked. Tears gathered on her lashes, spilling over as the silence stretched between them for several long seconds.

Matheus struggled to his feet, a pained groan escaping his lips. He faced her, his face set in a hard mask. "Ye will do as commanded."

"Nay," Meredith took a step back. "I willna condemn our people to a fate worse than death. There are other clans who we could make alliances with." Gritting her teeth, she narrowed her eyes and stared at her father, her chieftain.

"None as powerful–"

"Powerful?" Meredith shook her head. Dear god, when did they become so desperate as to forget the longstanding feud? "Before Caelan took over, there was honor in the Sinclair clan. They were fighters, but honest. All that has changed." Her flesh crawling, she clenched her fists. There were other clans, other men much more powerful. "Nay, he is not powerful. He uses the women and children as shields. How can such a man be considered an equal to ye, to our clan? Sinclair is weak, pathetic. Yet ye would bind me to his son for eternity to ease the burden on ye. I will find us an alliance which will see our people safe and whole."

"Ye will do nothing without my consent. Ye forget yer place, Meredith. I put the honor of the clan at the front of my mind."

"Yer consent? Ye forget who ye're speaking to. I am yer daughter and yet ye would trade me off as if I had no more value to ye than yer horse." Seething, Meredith exhaled sharply. "Clan Frazer willna bend to the whims of Sinclair or the English. I will never agree to such an alliance." Meredith stalked across the room and opened the door. "A flea-bitten mongrel dog would be a better match than a Sinclair, Papa. They will destroy what is left of yer legacy. Is that what ye desire, Papa?

"I want to know my clan will be taken care of when I pass. I wasna blessed with a son, Meredith. There is no heir apparent to take my place and see our people to prosperity."

"Nay, there is no son." Meredith lifted her chin, her throat tight, tears choking her. Her throat ached, the skin painfully tight. "Only the misbegotten daughter who stands before ye begging ye to think before ye agree to the marriage."

"My end is in sight, Meredith. I would have ye settled."

"Settled? Ye would have me–"

"Ye will do yer duty, Meredith. I will hear no more about this. Ye will agree to this union and we will see prosperity and security for our people."

"Nay, Papa, I will not simply settle. I will not wave aside the legacy of our ancestors or the wealth of our people. I will think of something, some means to save us all."

"I have failed ye, Meredith. It is my fault ye are so headstrong. A flaw I have nurtured and grown."

"Aye, it is a flaw to ye. I tell ye, my lord, do what ye must. I, however, will never submit to such a deal." Meredith inhaled a shaky breath. "I shall not rest until I do, Papa." Closing the door, Meredith leaned her forehead against the wood. A total disaster, 'twas what it was.

She had to find a way to protect them all. There had to be a clan who the Sinclairs feared. An alliance with them would surely send Sinclair and his bastard son scurrying into the wind.

It was the only way to ensure the Frasers survived.

Chapter Two

Ailen stomped down the steps to the courtyard, the cool air of a northern wind stirring the hem of his brat. "Damn blampots, do they na understand I have duties? Who are these fools?" Ailen shot a glance at his third in command, Charles.

"They didna say. I left them under the careful eye of Patrick and Miles."

"God above, there are more important matters to see to than some petty gossip. Edward approaches with only a thought to destroying us all and our neighbours want to stand about with wagging tongues." Ailen ground out through clenched teeth. He had little time for the folly of gossip from a neighbouring clan. As if there wasna enough conflict within the highlands, fools had to creep upon his doorstep and demand an audience.

The ever-present shadows of his two commanders Charles and Hugh did little to sooth the buzz of emotion beneath his skin. He kicked aside a clump of lingering ice, sending it skittering across the ground.

The late day sun cast shadows across the ground, wrapping around the two men hovering near their horses beneath two trees.

"What message did they bring?" Ailen shot a sharp glance over his shoulder at Hugh.

"We pressed them several times. Each time they claimed their Chieftain insisted they speak only to ye, Ailen."

He was not a politician; he was a warrior and stroking the egos of other clans did little to improve his mood. A stiff wind buffeted him as if to mirror his mood. Exhaling sharply, Ailen pushed aside any further thought. "It matters not, Hugh. It is a duty I despise, but we will hear what they have to say and make appropriate plans." Ailen shook his head and continued, hard heeled, toward the two men. "Well, what message do ye deliver to me?" He stopped an arm's length away from the pair.

"Apologies, sir," the younger of the two shifted uneasily. "But MacGreghere insisted."

MacGreghere? What did he want? The man was hell bent on eliminating any threat to his wife like some sotted fool. "Speak quickly. My patience is as thin as watered-down ale." Ailen gestured for the man to continue.

The elder of the pair ducked his head too slowly to hide the grin that tugged at his lips but held his tongue.

"Our Chieftain requests ye attend a special meeting. The threat of the English is not the only one we Highlanders face and he would come up with some plan before the English ride across our borders."

"There is but one means to solve the English problem. Why would he seek counsel with me?"

"He asks ye to meet him at Conach. It is on what is now MacGreghere lands. There are whispers that the Sinclairs are in alliance with the English."

"Those bastards are not worthy of a bag full of shite."

Ailen glanced at his second in command, one brow raised. "Sinclairs are cowards. With the old chieftain's death, any honor they had was cast aside. If they are in alliance with the English, then they deserve to burn in the depths of hell. However, nothing yet has made an attempt to clear up why MacGreghere wants me there. We are not allies."

"Ye are not enemies either." The elder of the pair interjected. "MacGreghere is only concerned with keeping mutual enemies under control. If the Sinclairs are in alliance with Edward's forces, it would allow them a clear path into the highlands.

"Still, I would know what he expects from me. I willna send my people to their death without a clear idea of what MacGreghere desires." Ailen stared at the MacGhregere clansman. "I am certain there is more to this message."

"Indeed." the man shifted. "I would reveal all that I was told." He cast a look at the men behind Ailen. "As instructed by my Chieftain. While I was not made privy to all the man's thoughts, it is clear there stands a risk to all clans. Not just ours if the Sinclairs are not put in their place."

"Speak clearly. Ye bore us with yer endless chatter."

"Charles," Ailen held up a hand, silencing the other man. "There is no love between many of the clans in the highlands. MacGreghere himself knows this. Only his marriage broke apart the feud between the Grahams and his clan. His disagreement with—"

"It is not MacGreghere's concern of the alliances within other clans, sir. In truth, I am not privy to his most inner thoughts." The man cleared his throat. "The Sinclairs have declared they will take on the Frazer clan. Their current leader has made claims his son is to wed Frazer's daughter. It is a move made only to usurp the old man's power. The Highland Frazers hold ties to the lowland clan and–"

"If the lowlander Frazers wish to keep their position, they must align with the English."

Ailen whirled around and glared at Hugh. "The lowland clans are closer to the English. It has been so for over a hundred years. Many of the noblemen from the lowlands are friendly with the English. It is how they keep their lands and their position. Allow him to speak so we may know all that he knows."

His men nodded and crossed their arms over their chests. Patrick shoved aside one of the other of Ailen's men and stepped into place at Ailen's shoulder. "We will hold questions until ye are done. Hold to the truth."

"I wouldna dishonour my clan by lying. It is the truth I have spoken, and the truth I will continue to speak."

"Very well." Satisfied, Ailen faced the messengers again. "So MacGreghere would have me move my men into position to attack the Frazers?"

"Nay. He said nothing about the Frazers beyond the Sinclairs forcing the old man into a union."

"Then what does he–"

"Charles." Ailen held up a hand. "Hold yer questions for now. Continue."

"Edward is even now growing stronger. MacGreghere would stop the bastards from invading the highlands and his clan. To do so, he wishes to speak to other chieftains to ensure that we show a united front to all. Most important of all, England. The discord among the clans is something all can agree on has been around for generations. It is more sport than anything at this point. England's interest in our lands, in our people, is far greater a risk."

"How many other clans has he sent word to?"

"Four, sir. He didna send a messenger to the Sinclairs or the Frazers, as neither has proven to be trustworthy. Chieftain MacGreghere has taken on the care of not only his clan but the Grahams as well. With both clans united, he has swelled our numbers. But it is not enough to stand against the bastard, Edward." The younger messenger blurted out. "He said Conach is the most neutral position."

Ailen scratched at his jaw. Knowing the strength of the enemy would work in their favor. Edward was power hungry, determined to break Scotland beneath his boot. There were those who trailed after him like well-trained whores, eager to take his leavings as if he had a true claim to Scotland. While the English king had not yet made it to the highlands, if there was not sufficient guard against such, he would.

The Highland Frazers were skilled and powerful. To his knowledge, they had no need of an alliance with anyone. Mathieus Frazer, while getting older, was still a man of sound mind. So why would the Sinclairs be so insistent?

To know the reason behind such an action would prove beneficial. Standing against Sinclairs would be an advantage they could use. If MacGreghere held some knowledge, they could use it against the bastard Sinclair. Aye, perhaps it was worth it to hear the other man out.

Ailen jerked his head at once. "Ye will have my answer shortly. Until then, accept my hospitality. Ye are welcome to food and drink. Rest."

"We thank ye, Chieftain."

"See to their needs, Bernard." Ailen looked at the hovering lad.

With a last glance at MacGreghere's messengers, Ailen stalked toward the barn, hands behind his back. Attending the meeting would give them information they could use. The safety of their clan was important. If there was a threat from outside as well as inside the Highlands, they needed to.

"Ailen, I dona think this is a wise decision. Our people wouldna stand a chance. If it is as the messenger says, perhaps MacGreghere's intent is to draw us into a plot and turn it against us." Charles spoke softly, his brow drawn down over his eyes. "It would be a fool's errand to let down our guard, one we canna afford."

"None of it makes sense. Sinclair's interest in Meredith Frazer strikes me as odd. The woman is not known for her beauty, plain in appearance. She was given free rein and treated much like he would a son. Opinionated, strong willed, with no resemblance to a proper lady. The Frazer lass is no delicate flower."

"She is the only child of Mathieus Frazer and grew up as wild as a horse. Plain or na' marrying her would put her husband into a position to take over the clan. Sinclair sees the wealth they have, as well as the ties to the lowlands, and to the English. If the rumours are true, by joining with her, he would have greater power to seduce the English with."

"The man would be daft to consider such a thing. There is hardly a thought of interest for the woman - only what she can bring to the marriage. It makes little sense. Less sense than why MacGreghere, a man who has become even more powerful since he married Elizabeth Graham, desire a meeting to contain–"

He shifted on his feet. Meredith's appearance aside, it made sense to bind her in marriage if one sought to gain more power. From what little he had heard of her, the woman was a sharp tongued mouse with nary a dowry to take to her marriage. Her father held so little hope of her finding a husband he had made no move to secure her a husband. Something or someone knew more than they spoke. The coming meeting would give answers. Ailen faced his men. "What purpose is there for the Sinclairs to take over the Frazers? There is something touched by the devil there. Everyone knows Caelan is a man with a mind only to his own wealth."

"Sinclairs are powerful. Their men are well trained. Not as well trained as ours, but they would be a formidable enemy."

"Aye, or allies."

"Do you believe MacGreghere would seek them out?"

Ailen snickered and shook his head. "The man is of a singular mind. Protect his clan and the highlands. He holds no love for any who would dare challenge his power, especially by using a woman. Nay, I fear there is something else he seeks." Ailen inhaled and gave a short nod. "We will meet with MacGreghere and the others. War haunts our steps and I would be prepared for it."

"When do you wish to leave?"

"At first light. Tell MacGreghere's men we depart with the rising of the sun," Ailen clapped Hugh on the shoulder. "Select a suitable guard and for the love of god, try not to speak of it to your wife. We doona need the entire clan to know anything until we have more information."

Hugh's cheeks darkened, and he bowed his head before striding off. Ailen watched him depart for a moment before turning to Charles and Patrick. "I would have you remain here. I dona believe our enemies would not march upon the undefended. If there is need, send word and we will return."

"MacGreghere is a man of honour," Patrick raked a hand through his hair. "Else he wouldna take in his wife's kin so readily."

"Honourable or not, I willna be content until we are back within the borders of our lands," Ailen retorted. "We shouldna be gone too long."

Chapter Three

Meredith chewed on the jagged edge of her thumbnail, her gaze locked on her father's hunched figure. Three other men sat with him, their heads bent together as if to prevent her from hearing their words.

It mattered little. The outcome would remain the same. She would not be beaten into a marriage to a monster.

Nay, she needed another, stronger man her father would not dare challenge to sway him from the path he walked upon. There were other clans stronger, but securing their agreement whilst still in her father's home proved a greater challenge.

Perhaps if she were to sneak away.

"They act as though ye have no ears."

"They pray I dona have them, or that I willna put up a ruckus when the time comes." Meredith turned, a small smile creeping across her face..The young maid's marriage was one of love and devotion. Secured with ease by a man within the clan. What did she know of alliances and loveless marriages? "Ah, but Abigail, it is my father's duty to secure my marriage. They do not seek to avoid it, only to get the most from Sinclairs."

"He agreed?" Abigail gasped, her eyes widening.

"Our Chieftain is an old man. His concerns are not for one but for all." Meredith faced the gathering again. It was misplaced as the Sinclair clan's honour had faded away with the wind. "Let them talk. It willna happen."

"If ye are commanded to marry, ye canna refuse."

Meredith dropped her hand. She clasped her hands together and faced the maid. "I dona dare defy our lord. He knows my stand on this matter."

"Do ye not want to marry? To have a husband and children?"

Meredith exhaled sharply. "Of course I wish for a husband, a family of my own. 'Tis not a matter of no desire to marry Abigail. It is a matter of who he would force me to wed."

"Some see yer actions as willful and proud. Ye shame yer father by yer refusal."

Heat blossomed in her chest. How dare anyone assume such a thing? "I am loyal to my father, to our people. If he did not wish me to have a mind, perhaps he should not have encouraged me when I was younger."

"Perhaps he didna think his efforts would be in vain."

"He knew." Meredith swallowed around the lump in her throat. With the death of her mother and younger brother, their fate had altered. Perhaps if he had wed again. She shook her head, pushing aside the train of thought. "What news do ye bring?"

"Johnas would speak with–"

Meredith's stomach twisted. "Yer brother has come seeking counsel with my father?" Pressing her hands together, Meredith lifted her fingers to her lips. What news could the young warrior be bringing to them? It could not be bad, else Abigail would have been quicker in speaking of his arrival. Perhaps it was nothing more than gossip from another clan - if so, could she use the information to suit her own purpose?

"Aye, he has gotten word of a gathering. I know nothing else, my lady," Abigail's brows drew together. "Why do you wear such a look? Ye plot something?"

"I canna plot anything, till I know what news he brings." Meredith patted the other woman's shoulder and gathered her skirts in hand. "Come, we will speak with yer brother. Let the old men plot against us for a while longer."

Meredith led the way from the hall toward the front of the stronghold. Her stomach lurched with each hurried step. The elders, nor her father wouldna well receive such disobedience. Her duty was to marry, to produce an heir for her husband - and it was one she would embrace.

If her husband were anyone but a Sinclair or an Englishman. A shudder raced along her spine. It appeared she would be saddled with both - or as close to as possible.

Sucking in a quick breath, Meredith slipped through the door. Hovering at the edge of the stone step, a robust young man waited. Long hair fell in waves past his shoulders, and the golden hint of a beard covered his jaw.

"Johnas, welcome." Meredith stepped forward, hand outstretched. The young warrior turned and faced her.

"Lady Meredith." He bowed his head to her. "I have come with news for yer father."

"He is in council at the moment and would not be disturbed. Come, come. Abigail fetch a glass of ale and something to eat," Meredith swept a hand toward the corridor. "Whilst Pappa is in council, there is no reason for ye to stand about absent refreshments."

Johnas shot a look at Abigail and nodded. "Ye are too kind, my lady."

"Ye are kin. Come, rest by the fire," Meredith led the way into a smaller chamber and gestured to a tall chair by the fire. "I hope the news is not too harsh. Chieftain Frazer's mind is so focused on the unpleasantness with England."

Johnas settled in the seat and chuckled. "I am aware of where his mind wanders these days. The highlands are abuzz with word of yer upcoming marriage."

Meredith clenched her teeth. Of course, the news had spread. Damn the Sinclairs to the depths of Hell. "What news do ye bring? Ye wouldna be here to discuss my upcoming union." The words lay sour on her tongue and gulped back the bitterness scalding her throat.

"Should we wait?–"

Meredith bit back a curse. Any delay would leave her no time to plan around the news. If it were bad, she would need to soften it. If it were something she could use, then she would need time to plan. "It is best not to," Meredith waved aside her servant's suggestion with a careful smile. "I imagine it is timely."

"Indeed."

Meredith caught the barest of movements in the corner of her eye before Abigail appeared with bread and cheese and a cup of ale. She gave it to Johnas and stepped back. "I would not press ye, but if yer message is timely, perhaps ye could speak it whilst ye eat?"

Johnas lifted the cup to his lips, gulping at the liquid before lowering his hand and wiping his face on his sleeve. "There is to be a meeting. MacGreghere has called for several of the other clans to meet with him."

"Are we expected to attend?" Abigail's voice wavered. "The man isna known for his acceptance of other–"

Meredith rolled her eyes. Rumors and lies had done nothing to ease the fear many still held for Callum McGreghere. "Abigail, the man is not a monster. He didna slaughter the Grahams after he wed Elizabeth. He hunted down the Stewarts and her brother, aye, but he had cause to." Meredith shot her maid a harsh look. "Johnas, please, continue."

"The four clans he invited are to meet at Conach in four days' time. They are to discuss several things. Wallace's movement, as well as the current situation with the Sinclairs, and, of course, the English."

"Aye, MacGreghere has no love for the English. And who counts the Sinclairs as friend these days? Do ye know who was summoned?"

"I have been told the Lindsay clan will be in attendance, as will the Dunbars, and I am uncertain of the others. My lady, I should speak no more of this without yer father's presence."

Meredith nodded. Johnas had given her more than he intended - and every bit of the news could be used for their purposes. Those set to gather could offer the reward she sought. If memory served, the Dunbars were a smaller clan but by no means weak or easily pushed around. In their favor, they opposed the Sinclairs, but would hold little threat against the other clan. If memory serves, their Chieftain was also wed with two young sons. Lindsay's clan leader was feared by many of the highland clans. His reputation preceded him as a man ruthless in his pursuits.

If she could convince one of them to play along with her ruse…

Oh, but how? The trip to Conach would take at least a day of heavy riding, and she didna know who else would be in attendance.

Could she risk not going? If she didna go, she stood to lose a chance to get an ally for her cause. Were those who were summoned against the Sinclairs or for?

"Ye wear yer thoughts upon yer face, my lady," Johnas chuckled. "If ye plan to attend, then ye must be aware none are friends with the Sinclairs. And the Frazer name is not well received either. Our lowland cousins have not made us any friends."

Her cheeks burning, Meredith lowered her head. "Forgive me."

"I will say only this," Johnas got to his feet. "If ye plan on anything, make excuses and depart quickly. Ye may find an ally within the group, willing to hear yer thoughts."

"Johnas, hold yer tongue," Abigail hissed. "Lady Meredith dona do anything foolish. It is best to speak to Chieftain Frazer first, before ye do anything."

"Put yer mind at ease, Abigail. I will do nothing without proper consideration." Meredith smiled at the other woman and strode from the room. Abigail was a dear friend, but she had no idea of how lucky she was. Her future was set. The children she would bear and raise for her husband were more than simply pawns in a larger game.

Nay, Meredith shook her head. She wouldna allow her father to be cheated out of what was rightfully his.

This meeting would give her a chance, however, impossible, to seek aid and garner a strong friend. She would be careful and it would be perfect. Two of her most trusted guards would accompany her on the journey to Conach. There she would secure the alliance her father needed without having to endure being married.

The Sinclairs would never lay claim to the Frazer clan's lands, the people. Nothing would be forfeited. She would see them free of Sinclair's demands.

Her heart tightened briefly. The prospect of marriage was not what frightened her. Meredith forced herself to calm her racing heart. Nay, she longed for a husband, for children… but not because it was the only way to protect her people.

A marriage of love, of devotion, aye, those were the dreams she had yet clung to. Oh, how she wanted more than duty. Meredith gave herself a quick shake and straightened. Time wouldna pause, her departure would need to be swift, and her father made none the wiser.

~*~

High stone fences encircled a simple stone and sod cottage with a larger stone house beyond it. Two smaller lean-tos held horses. Throughout the yard, trees clawed their way up through rocky ground. Among them, fires dotted the yard of the small bailey. The waning light seduced by the promise of night as Meredith swung down from the saddle. Horses stood tethered under several trees near the stone wall next to the larger round house.

Men shuffled between the fires. Raucous laughter and the clatter of weapons, a dull roar she could not decipher past the thundering echo of her pulse in her ears. Narrow-eyed, she cast a slow glance over the gathering. There was nary a single familiar face. Swords and spears, armour, and leather.

Behind her, the two seasoned warriors she had coerced into attending her on her mission approached. She glanced over her shoulder as they stopped at her side.

"There are at least twenty warriors present, my lady. Several I have not seen before." One guard, an older man with greying hair at the temples and crow's feet near his eyes, leaned toward her. The low rumble of his voice barely penetrated the throbbing of her pulse in her ears.

"Then it will be easier for us to sneak in, Angus. We do not need to be delayed unduly."

Angus shot the other guard a look and exhaled. "Lady Meredith, those gathered will not look kindly upon having a woman intrude on their gathering. Women dona belong in talks of war. 'Tis better ye let us handle the matter."

Wiping her sweaty palms on her brat, Meredith exhaled a shaky breath. They didna know the full measure of her intent and she wouldna ask more than she already had. If there were consequences, let her face them alone. "I must be present," her voice crackling Meredith waved aside his concern. She scanned those gathered through narrowed eyes. "The plan is risky enough, as is. Failing is going to result in far more than my wounded pride."

"MacGreghere, Lindsay, Dunbar, McLeod, Campbell - some of the most powerful clans are here. None of whom are allied with yer father."

"Aye, I recognize one from the Graham clan."

"They are part of MacGreghere's forces."

Meredith's gaze caught on a tall, broad-shouldered man with long brown hair. Jutting above his right shoulder, the hilt of a sword caught the flickering hold of the flames as he strode between two roaring fires. Scarred knees peeked from beneath his lien and brat.

He turned, narrowed eyes scanning the gathering. He paused, his eyes locked with hers, and Meredith shivered. The dim brogue of her guards faded into nothing as she stared across the yard.

Her heart skittered in her chest. She swallowed, her tongue working against the roof of her mouth. Her stomach leapt into her throat. A thousand wings fluttered beneath her skin.

Meredith moistened her lips with her tongue, the stranger's stare following the motion. He straightened, a slow curl of his lips upward.

One of the men with him spoke to him and he half turned to him. The movement cast his profile in the light. A thin scar crossed his face from his ear to his nose, the skin puckered along the ragged line. The muscles in his jaw moved, and he spoke. The man he addressed nodded and stepped back.

Between one beat of her heart and the next, the movement of the camp shifted, and he vanished in the crowd. Meredith stood, her heart pounding, her blood racing through her veins. She stepped to one side, searching for him.

Wilting beneath the weight of her own disappointment, Meredith huffed a breath. Had she found him?

Chapter Four

Meredith paced the confines of the narrow space between two stone walls, her gaze darting through the shadows. There was little to be done until her guards returned with word from the Chieftains gathered.

Surely, they would see the value in the offered alliance. Four hundred trained soldiers to be called upon was no small thing. The warriors would prove of benefit in light of the conflict her kin from the borderlands had spoken of.

A branch cracked, and she whirled, her heart in her throat. Two figures moved toward her, their familiar features easing the tension in her throat.

"Well? Did they find our offer enticing?" Meredith cast a quick glance between the two men.

"My lady, ye must ken they are warriors."

"Aye, and four hundred of our men would be of use upon the battlefield." She flexed her fingers, her hands itching to grab hold of the two men and shake them. "Are we not at war? What clan can afford to turn away aide by a well-trained–"

"My lady," Angus raised a hand, halting her speech. "MacGreghere has ample trained men. In fact, all gathered have ties to one another in some way. In truth, they hold no interest in an army and ye have offered nothing more."

"I can offer nothing more without our Father's permission."

"Ye can offer nothing without his consent, my lady. In truth, he knows nothing of our presence and he may be sorely put out—"

"Father is in no state to make such a decision, Baird," Meredith hissed through clenched teeth. "And I willna stand for a union with the Sinclairs. They are little more than animals. Nay, there must be something we can offer that will be enticing."

The two men glanced at each other, the matching frowns and the way they avoided her gaze, leaving her with ice in her veins. "If ye have something to say dona, let yer pride hold yer tongue." Meredith narrowed her eyes. Their hesitancy spoke volumes, and none of which she wanted to hear. "Speak freely."

"My lady, of those gathered there are but two who would offer protection from the Sinclairs. Neither is eager nor willing to speak to ye. Not with the offer ye put forward. They are men, warriors, and whilst shoring up their forces would be welcomed, 'tis not enough. There is no love for the Frazer clan. Many have heard the whispers and rumors, or more damning perhaps, know of the lowland Frazers."

Her stomach dropped to her feet. Good lord, fools and bampots. There wasna anything she could do about her kin and their foolishness with the English. Nay, she could only focus on the here and now. Her people didna deserve to be under the heel of the Sinclairs. "What would entice them to hear me out?"

"Ye are a woman, my lady."

"I am aware. What does such a thing have to do with the predicament we are in?"

"Unions between clans are delicate matters. Yer father wouldna agree to just any alliance and most of those gathered are already wed."

Meredith gasped. Surely he didna mean? Nay, she had to have misheard him. "Have ye lost yer mind?"

Baird sighed and crossed his arms over his chest. "My lady, there is little else we can say. In truth, if ye wish to see this union between ye and the Sinclair lad abandoned, ye need to find another husband. Ye offer soldiers in a time of war. But to entice them further, ye may need to resort to more. Ye have a most impressive dowry."

Or at least one willing to play the part. Meredith turned away, a chill racing through her. She dared not fail. Could one of these men be convinced to assist in a much needed ruse? If she were already wed, her father wouldna be held responsible for the breaking of the betrothal. Aye, it could work. A soft wind stirred the hair at her temple and she reached up to push it aside. Who could she convince to play along with the plot? Her guard spoke of two Chieftains. If they were allied with MacGreghere, it was likely they were powerful. More powerful than Sinclair, she couldna say.

But they need not be more than Sinclair. They need only be so powerful as to stand against the bampots. Aye, it could work - if there was fitting compensation.

"Who among those gathered is powerful enough to put a halt to the fool's errand?" Meredith lifted her hand to her lips, biting at the edge of a nail. "He need not do anything but go along with ruse until Father and Sinclair yield to the folly and move on."

"I doubt any of the men gathered would be willing to partake of yer deceit."

A slow rolling brogue carried to her and Meredith blinked. Her heart pounding, she stepped closer to the stone wall. Two men strode into view and her heart jumped. She grasped the cold stones and allowed a small smile to touch her lips. (Insert name's) voice faded into the night and she bit back a laugh. He had been an imposing figure.

"What of the man they follow?" She half turned to meet her guard's gaze. "They were with him earlier, tall, brown hair past his shoulders."

"Lindsay clan members," Angus scratched at his jaw. "They willna help ye."

Her pulse skittered, and she turned back to watch the men vanish into the shadows. Lindays were feared by many of the clans. The new leader was a man of few words and a fierce temper. Her father's voice whispered in her ear. A long-winded discussion on the Lindsay clan and how even though they werena enemies of her clan, they werena friends either. Nay, to consider him would be to invite disaster.

"They dona need to do anything," Meredith sucked in a deep breath. Like a spark from blade against stone, hope fluttered to life within her chest. The Lindsay Chieftain would prove to be her best choice. If she could get him to–Whirling, she faced her guard. "Find the Lindsay Chieftain. I would speak with him."

"My lady, he willna speak to ye." Angus shook his head. "'Tis a waste of time. I say we return home. Perhaps yer father will have thought—"

"I didna ask ye to find him. 'Tis a command I give. Bring the man to me so I may speak with him. The fate of our clan depends on my success."

"Lady Meredith, Angus is right. Ailen Lindsay willna speaks to ye even if he were to grant ye an audience. We be Frazers and our clan name's reputation precedes us. If ye wish to have any success, ye will need to think of another means."

A dull throbbing behind her eyes spread into a sharper ache and she rubbed at her temple. If he wouldna be willing to meet with her, then she would relieve him of choice. Her father's future, her entire clan's future, was at stake. None ken what it meant if they all fell. MacGreghere's taking over the Graham clan had been peaceful. Sinclair's takeover would end with bloodshed. Nay, she would need to think of another means, one that if need be, she would swallow her pride.

Too many times she had been the one deciding, the choices. Lady of the house had blended into acting as her father's heir. Meredith straightened and exhaled. She wouldna stand by idly while the work they had done crumbled.

"If he willna come willingly," Meredith raised a brow. "Drag him. He is our last hope. Casting aside the chance is not an option."

"Aye, if ye were but a man, my lady, there would be nary a clan to stand against us," Baird chuckled. "There are more of them than there are of us, my lady. The gathering will end soon and perhaps that will be our chance. Chieftain Lindsay travels with two guards. Should there be an incident on the trail?"

Meredith exhaled sharply. It was sound logic, Baird offered, but she wasna interested in starting a war with the Lindsay clan. Any move they made had to be before they left the gathering. Raucous laughter drifted on the breeze and she froze. Those gathered spoke at length, plied with wine and ale. Patience would garner her a better opportunity to speak with him.

Aye, she would wait until the right moment.

"We need not resort to such an underhanded and cowardly means," Meredith nodded and lifted her hand to her lips. The slow glide of a nail between her teeth soothed the butterflies gathering in her belly. "The night is young, and the ale flows. We will wait until he has withdrawn from the meeting." She wouldna fail.

~*~

"What have ye learned?" Ailen lifted the simple cup of ale to his lips and took a slow drink, his gaze locked on the figure hiding within the shadows.

"Nothing. She is unknown to those gathered. It was thought perhaps she was part of the McGreghere's entourage, but he denies knowing her," Patrick lowered his voice. "Her guard has approached the other chieftains with an offer of an alliance."

"None have taken her offer?"

"Nay," Patrick was quick to reply. "I dona know who would send a woman to negotiate an alliance, but surely they would send more than two men to guard her."

"She is a Frazer," Hugh spoke around the crust of bread in his mouth. "Her offer of alliance is for soldiers in exchange for protection from Sinclair."

"I thought they had an arrangement between them." Movement across the yard drew his attention, and he straightened. The flickering of the fires cast eerie shadows across the young lass's figure as she moved from the safety of the wall to where the horses stood.

Slim, with long flowing hair that teased her backside, she moved with a confidence he couldna help but take note of. Was she the one he had seen earlier? Pale eyes in a round face, attempting to hide behind two burly soldiers.

"Aye, so the Sinclair Chieftain and his son claim. I wouldna put it past him to lie."

"Frazers canna be trusted, either. They are in bed with Edward, the English bastard."

"Matheus wouldna send his people to ruin with such an alliance. He despises the English as much as any who stand Scots," Patrick shook his head. "Sinclair has left the man with little room to maneuver. If he doesna wed his daughter to the Sinclairs, then they will overrun the Frazers."

Neither clan was worth much note. The lowland Frazers' alliance and acceptance of Edward to keep their lands and titles had left a foul taste on everyone's tongue. And the Sinclairs. Ailen shuddered, the contents of his stomach rolling in his gut. They were worse. The current chieftain was a man of little honour, a liar, and a thief. There were few in the Highlands who would give him a thought. Hell, if the man were standing before him on fire, Ailen wouldna spit on him.

"What words has she broken with the others?" Ailen set aside his empty cup and followed the woman's movements with his gaze. "What exactly was she offering?"

"They have four hundred able men. A hefty number, but they are not equal to our forces." Patrick gestured across the yard. "I wouldna trust them, not if her father is willing to send a woman to do his negotiating."

Ailen glanced at his warrior, a muscle flexing in his jaw. "If it is as you say, who else would he send? She is his only heir."

"She is a woman, prone to illogical and unsound decisions," Patrick huffed. "No matter what she offers, it wouldna be enough to convince any reasonable man to accept the alliance."

Ailen exhaled sharply and faced the other man. Meredith Frazer showed more courage than most men to attend such a meeting with only two guards. He would not see her name sullied without reason. "Because she is a woman? Or because she is a Frazer?"

"Neither is appealing, my lord."

"It matters not, Ailen, with the lack of response, she will be gone with the morning light." Hugh shoved Patrick aside with a harsh look. "We have had dealings with the Frazer clan before. It didna go well. I believe there was bloodshed."

God above, yes. Three summers before, one farmstead at the edge of his territory had been attacked by several Frazers. The farmer had been killed, his two daughters stolen away.

"Aye. Fool has no recollection of the attack. Should send her head back upon a–"

"Watch yer tone, Patrick. She may be a Frazer, but there is sand in her. Far more than in most," Ailen ground out. "For now, ye will put such talk from yer minds. We have much to do before we return home. The Frazer lass willna approach us - and I wouldna spend time debating her motives. Callum will seek a final meeting before we leave tomorrow. I would have ye both well rested. The enemy is not a slip of a girl, but the English who creep every closer to our lands and those who would aid them. Not to mention the treacherous Scots with an eye on destroying everyone and everything outside their lands."

"I will remain on guard, Patrick," Hugh glared at Patrick. "Less the wee lass raises an army between now and the dawn."

Patrick glared at the other man as he shouldered Hugh from his path. He sank to the ground by his saddle and rolled over to put his back to the far stone wall. "I do not fear the woman, Hugh. I simply do not trust her not to be like her kin."

"Patrick," Ailen's voice cut through the air like a blade, and the other man snorted before curling up and pulling his brat tighter around him.

"He is young, Ailen. Eager to see ye to safety and away from temptation." Hugh moved closer, dropping his voice to a harsh whisper. "'Tis the truth, Patrick had kin who were treated poorly by the Frazers. He may hold her responsible."

"The lass has done nothing."

"She attends a meeting her clan was not invited to. Is that not reason enough for suspicion?"

"Aye, her clan wasna invited. In truth, if McGreghere were to know of her presence, there would be hell to pay. She has gumption," Ailen chuckled and raked a hand through his hair. "Tell me, Hugh, if ye wer being told to wed Sinclair's bastard son, would ye not do the same?"

Hugh laughed and clapped him on the shoulder. "Indeed. I wouldna force him on a dog, much less me daughter. Take to yer pallet, sir. The morn comes quickly."

Chapter Five

His skull throbbing painfully, Ailen groaned and rolled over. He blinked, the light from the dawn clawing at his eyes. Each movement worsened the pounding in his head, and he groaned. He swallowed, his mouth dry.

Ailen raised a hand to his head as he sat up slowly. What in God's name had he drunk the night before?

"My lady, he wakes." Unfamiliar, the masculine voice preceded the rushed steps approaching.

He forced his eyes open, squinting against the harsh glare of the light. Two mildly familiar men stood at the edge of the stone wall, hands on their swords. Movement beyond them drew his eye and he bit back a curse.

"Patrick appears to be–"

"You awaken." In a flurry of brat and hair, the lass hunkered at his feet. "Angus, get him water to clear his head." She offered a small smile. "A thousand apologies, Chieftain…"

"Lindsay." The older guard appeared behind her with a cup. "My lady, water."

She reached up and took it before offering it to him. "Here, it is safe."

"Safe? What cause could there be to think it safe, my lady? You have obviously–"

"Nay, it was not I who causes discomfort in your head or mouth full of wool. That is the ale. It pains me to rely on such as this to ensure a meeting. Desperate measures, sir, require desperate actions."

Ailen glanced around. The stone wall stood tall, with nary a stone missing. Beyond it, a small hut sat darkened. Three horses stood in front of the building. Rushing water filled his ears, and an icy fist closed around his throat. "I am no longer in–"

"Nay, ye are not." A younger guard stepped forward, his arms crossed over his chest. "I do not see the value of keeping him alive, my lady. He willna aid you."

"Baird, please," she twisted, balancing herself with a hand on Ailen's ankle. Sparks danced across skin beneath her hand, heating his blood, and Ailen swallowed hard. "He has not heard my offer and I would have his refusal to come from Chieftain Lindsay's lips."

Baird snorted and strode several strides away. Feet braced, he waved a hand at her.

"Forgive my guard. I wanted a few moments of yer time, sir. I am Meredith Frazer, daughter of Mathieus Frazer and our clan is under threat by a common enemy." She blinked, tears gathering on her lashes for a moment before she fought them back. A faint quiver in her voice belied the emotions she hid from him. "A threat I would see removed from both of our clans."

"He canna be much of an enemy if ye are betrothed to him." Ailen gathered himself and stood, dislodging her hand. A shiver raced along his nerves at the loss of warmth. She was only a mortal woman, one who would see him a fool if he didna take care.

She stared up at him, tendrils of hair falling around her face. Dark smudges beneath her eyes spoke of sleepless nights. She licked her lips and struggled to her feet. "Aye, 'tis a demand he made of my father and chieftain, but it is not a union either of us seeks." She clasped her hands before her. "My clan has something Sinclair desires, and he is willing to do anything to get it."

"What is it you think he desires? A new wife in his bed is often enough of a temptation."

Color flooded her face and Meredith's lower lip trembled, but she didna look away. Holding his gaze, she continued as if he hadna spoken. "I have long known my father would ensure an alliance by marriage. It is a duty I would see done. But this is not what my father desires, nor an arrangement he needs. Sinclair sees his chance to usurp my father and secure an alliance with England. He doesna desire me - only what he can get with the union. It is not a fate I would see my people, or any other clan, too. Unlike my kin in the lowlands, we are Highlanders. Our loyalty is to ourselves, to Scotland."

"Brave words, my lady, but I am uncertain I understand yer purpose to the current situation." He waved a hand at the meager surroundings. "Ye stole me from a conference–"

"Indeed, we did. Perhaps ye would shut up and let my lady speak." Angus shifted, the clink of his sword loud in the stillness. "I have no desire to linger."

"Angus, there is no need to prod the man. 'Tis my fault for the delay. I have prattled on needlessly." Meredith's tone was sharp, unyielding. "Chieftain Lindsay, to ensure that my clan doesna suffer a far less pleasant fate than the Graham clan, I would propose an alliance."

"Four hundred–"

"Nay, warriors dona seem to be of any interest. While my soldiers are well trained, I fear they wouldna be well received. I have a far more intriguing offer for ye." Meredith pressed a hand to her lips for a moment. "To ensure the Sinclairs dona get anything, an alliance is not optimal. Nay, they can simply say the betrothal still stands. It must be something of substance."

Like rain dripping from the roof, a gnawing uncertainty filled Ailen's mind as he stared at her. It only increased when she began pacing in front of him. What madness could the lass have come up with? A glance at the two guards showed an echoing unease on their faces.

Meredith whirled to face him, hands flexing in front of her. "'Tis the only way."

"My lady?" Baird cleared his throat. "What plot have ye come up with?"

Meredith stepped closer to Ailen, her warm breath ghosting over the bare skin at his throat. She held his stare head on, a flash of something in her eyes he didna recognize, but instinct told him wouldna be anything he wanted to deal with. "Sinclair demands my hand in marriage - to escape such a fate, there is but one way. Chieftain Lindsay, ye will have to marry me."

Her guards' shouting barely penetrated the roaring in his ears as he gaped at her. "Forgive me, my lady, but I must have misheard ye."

"It wouldna be a real marriage. Only a ruse. In exchange for yer cooperation, ye would be given Oich creek."

"Lady Meredith, ye canna give away the–"

Meredith shot her guard a harsh glare. Her father had gifted it to her as dowry, she could and would do whatever she wished with it. "There is a small farmstead at the edge of the creek that runs through a fair clearing perfect for farming. See yer way to partake of this ruse and I shall see to it the land is gifted to ye."

A spark of admiration hit and Ailen tilted his head as he listened to her offer. A thread of steel ran through her voice, any trace of fear or discomfort well hidden. A rarity for a woman, most were emotional, illogical creatures prone to weeping at a moment's notice.

He knew the area she spoke of. It was rich farmland. There had been a time when his ancestors had wanted the land to expand their reach and create more distance between them and the McLean clan.

To get it would be a bounty for his people.

The land would be worth most anything. Her desperation, however, spoke to something far deeper. Something that prodded at his conscience. Meredith Frazer's offer held danger not only to his people but to his heart - if he were to let her yield the power any woman held.

"Ye offer me much, Lady Frazer. However, have ye put yer mind to the thought I may already be betrothed?"

She blinked at him, her eyes widening for a moment before she seemed to deflate a little. Meredith pressed her hands to her lips as if in thought before she straightened. "'Tis true the thought didna cross my mind."

"My lady, if it is as he says, and he is betrothed, then we need to find another option. Yer father willna wait much longer to send men after ye." Angus shared a glance with Baird. "He will be sorely put out and may hasten the marriage as punishment."

"Our kin in the lowlands may have sold their souls, but we have not. Pappa will understand." Meredith ground out through clenched teeth. "I will see myself free of this unwanted burden. If Chieftain Lindsay is to be wed, then we will simply find another means to ensure all benefit is given. It is not an actual marriage I spoke of, only a ruse until that bastard turns his attention elsewhere."

"Ye dona like the Sinclairs, my lady?"

"Nay, I dona care for them at all." Wide blue eyes stared at him, dark lashes fanning out over her cheeks. Soft, with a bit of roundness to them, a hint of colour blossomed the longer he stared. Freckles danced across the pale expanse of her nose and cheeks. Plump lips glistened with moisture when she licked them. Long, dark hair fell past her shoulders, draping across the ample softness of her bosoms. Her brat was tucked in around her waist, accentuating the flare of her hips.

Meredith wasna a mouse. Any man would need only look to see the beauty clinging to her. His fingers itched to reach out and touch, to see if the skin of her neck was as soft as it appeared. Ailen reached out, capturing a lock of hair between his fingers, and let it trail across his skin. Sparks raced along his nerves as the silky strands flowed through his grip.

He heard the rapid inhalation and paused. Nay, he wouldna agree to her terms. Crossing his arms over his chest, Ailen walked around her. "So ye propose an agreement which would benefit me greatly. What would ye get from it?" He leaned in closer, dropping his voice to a near whisper.

Her guards stepped forward, bristling, their hands on their swords. She raised her hand, halting them. "Freedom from the threat of Sinclair. The simple life my people know and enjoy within a threat hanging over their heads." A tremble raced along her voice, and he hid a smile.

"'Tis truly a bounty, ye offer. One far too large for such a small reward, my lady."

Meredith straightened and faced him. Her cheeks were stained a deep red, and storm clouds gathered in her eyes. The barest hint of temper flashing before it was masked. An oddity in a woman. "'Tis enough to know my people willna be destroyed. Our warriors willna be sent off to be slaughtered while our women made sport of. Chieftain Lindsay, a bit of land, some water - what value does it hold against the wellbeing of six hundred people?"

"Depends on who ye put the question to, Lady Meredith." Ailen stepped back and continued a slow, careful pace around her. "Six hundred is a number, one which contradicts what I understand to be on offer. Ye offered four hundred warriors, didna ye?"

"We have more men than women in our clan," Meredith admitted. "Women from my clan tend to marry into other clans. 'Tis nothing shameful or secret. Many women marry men not from their clan."

"Four hundred. How many have seen battle? How many of these men ye claim to have are older than thirteen summers?" Ailen pressed her. If memory served, Mathieus' forces were not so high. At last count, if he recalled, there were closer to two hundred seasoned soldiers. Had Mathieus sent his daughter to fool those who didna know their state? If so, the old man would pay dearly for such trickery.

"Lindsay, ye will no, batter her with yer words. Lady Meredith offers four hundred—"

"Angus, place tongue behind teeth." Ailen shot him a hard look. "'Tis a fair question, Lady Meredith. Ye offer a bounty to me in exchange for silence on yer plot. I simply wish to—"

"My father insists boys begin to train when they reach ten summers." Meredith licked her lips, her gaze dropping. "There are less than four hundred who are over the age of thirteen."

"And ye would send a boy of ten–"

"Nay," Meredith clenched her teeth, tears gathering on her lashes. "I would see the boys in the fields, to their training. I wouldna see any of my people marched off to battle if I could prevent it. My father knows there is little hope after our lowland kin sided with the English and Sinclair sniffing at our door. He knows everyone is against us and sees no way out. I would honour him and my clan by not seeing the ground stained with their blood. Is the land not enough? I have gold to offer. Perhaps some salt, but that is all." Her voice cracked and something within Ailen's chest tightened.

"Lady Meredith," Baird stepped forward, a scowl twisting his face. "Come, let us return home. Ye tried. Lindsay isna interested."

Meredith shook her head, a lone tear tracking down her cheek. She wiped it away and nodded. "Aye. Fetch our horses, Baird. I would be away."

Her guards nodded and headed for the horses, leaving her standing alone amid the small yard. Meredith shot him a look, the agony in her gaze pierced through to his heart, a sharp stab of emotion as he choked back.

Back straight, shoulders wide, Meredith turned and followed her guard. Pride and steel ran through her. Hell, Meredith Frazer was nothing like he expected. Instead of a mouse, he had stumbled across a wildcat.

If she were a man, she'd be unstoppable.

Ailen narrowed his eyes. Hell. He was a fool.

"Yer terms are admirable." Ailen grabbed her arm and pulled her back against him. "Yet I would offer my own." The warmth of her body pressed against his, the soft curve of her arse against his groin stirred the embers of lust.

Meredith yanked her arm free of his grasp and faced him. She glared at him through narrowed eyes, silent tears staining her cheeks. "Ye will aid us?" Meredith sniffled and wiped at the tears on her face. "My offer is–"

"In a manner of speaking." Ailen chuckled. Aye, he was a fool, but the reward would be worth the cost. "I will agree to yer offer. Yer clan warriors, the land…and you."

Meredith gasped and took a step back. "Me?"

The tiny squeak in her voice spoke volumes to him. "Aye," Ailen met her wide-eyed stare. "Lady Meredith. I will accept yer generous offer but the ruse willna stand. I would see my word honoured. I have no need of yer gold or yer salt, though the latter would be well received. I will take all ye offer as dowry to bring to our marriage."

Her lips parted on a soundless gasp, Meredith stared at him. She blinked, her cheeks darkening slightly. "I didna offer—"

Ailen shook his head. He allowed a small, slow smile to tease his lips. "Nay, ye didna. Ye gave yer terms, I give mine. I will ensure the Sinclairs leave yer clan alone. In exchange, ye will be my wife."

"I…I" Meredith raised a hand to her lips, chewing on her thumbnail. "Pappa willna permit such a thing."

Ailen chuckled and leaned closer, "Yer father will honour our agreement, Lady Meredith. I dona take him to be a fool. He is a man of his or rather in this instance yer word, even in his long years. He will plot against it but will agree to it in appearance at least. Yer bargain benefits me more than it does ye."

"It is a simple ruse. A falsehood told to turn a mutual enemy from their plans. Not an arrangement for marriage, sir."

"It is a proposal. Ye have given yer terms, I have given mine. What do ye say?" His lips brushed against her ear as he spoke. A shiver raced through her body and he grinned. Lady Meredith Frazer wasna as hard as she appeared. She licked her lips, and he followed the movement carefully. "Aye, I have yer answer. Good morn, Lady Meredith."

Chapter Six

Every muscle frozen, Meredith stared at the man in front of her. Her skin prickled as if poked by a thousand thorns and she shuffled a step away. "Ye canna be serious. Ye would break yer betrothal unnecessarily. Surely yer wife to be willna be pleased to be cast aside so readily."

Ailen shrugged one shoulder and crossed his arms over his chest.

Meredith gaped at him. "Ye would risk war with her clan? 'Tis no way ye would do such a thing. Ye know I dona expect ye to actually wed me." Cursing the break in her voice, Meredith bit down on the tip of her thumb. Good lord, it was a simple ruse. "I will give ye the land, the gold, the salt. All will be delivered to the cottage before ye reach yer—"

Ailen chuckled and glanced behind her. "Yer expectations are too low, my lady. Ye offer me a bounty many in the Highlands would kill for. Sinclair, by yer own, admission is willing to destroy your people for what ye offer. I dona think it is so farfetch'd. Ye have given me yer terms, Lady Meredith, and I have given ye mine." A hard, distant look erased any trace of mirth as he met her stare. "If ye want my assistance, ye know the cost."

"It is a price too high. For a simple ruse, a short time in which to settle the Sinclairs in their place." Meredith protested, her heart thundering against her ribs. He jested. It was the only explanation she could come up with.

"Nay, my lady, 'tis a fair offer - and a fair counter offer. The lives of my men are valuable, and Sinclair willna be eager to turn from his purpose. Blood will be spilt on both sides. Consider yer position with care, Lady Meredith." He stepped around her, his hand brushing across her waist, and stalked toward the stand of trees where the horses stood. Panic flared, a hot grip around her throat, and she whirled.

Surely he didna think her such a fool to believe he would risk angering another clan to save Baird, and Angus watched carefully as he swung atop the horse they'd put him on to bring him to the meeting. He half twisted in the saddle and met her eyes before he nudged the animal into a lope.

Heart pounding, Meredith swayed on her feet. Chieftain Frazer wouldna be forgiving if it was all for naught. Could she bear the cost if she didna honour her word? Ailen was correct. Sinclair would destroy her clan without mercy or a thought to the lives he tore asunder. She shuddered, her skin crawling at the idea of his bastard son's touch. Acair was nearly as vile as his father. Many women suffered beneath his control.

To save the many, she would sacrifice anything.

"My lady?" Angus cleared his throat. "What could he have said in such a short time?"

"I have secured our clan's freedom from Sinclairs." Meredith rubbed her hands on her brat. "I ride to Oich Creek immediately. Ye will send Baird to seek a priest and then ye will fetch Ailen Lindsay. I will meet ye both at the farmstead."

"My lady, ye didna do anything rash, did ye? Yer father is going to be furious when he learns of what ye have orchestrated."

"My father is of little concern at the moment," Meredith strode toward her horse. The means to secure their clan's future lay within grasp. She would deliver on her promise and perhaps Ailen wouldna force her hand. Let him think she considered his proposal - but she wouldna bind him to her. His help would be enough.

"I didna hear what he said, but saw yer reaction. Ye dona trust a man who would make the colour flee from yer face."

Nay, one shouldna trust such a man - but Ailen Lindsay was different. He offered her more than she asked. She exhaled. "Nay, one shouldna do so. Ailen Lindsay merely shocked me, he would ask for nothing I willna consider giving." Meredith stopped near her horse's head. The grey swung around, eyes wild and tossed his head. She collected the reins, gathered her leine, and put one foot in the stirrup. Angus appeared at her side and lifted her into the saddle. She settled on her skittish mount, settling it with a smack to the flank. "I have given ye instructions. See, they are carried out. Dona delay, Angus. I will expect ye all quickly."

"My lady. Consider yer actions for a moment. Yer father willna be pleased. Sinclairs will be furious. Any deal ye have struck will bring discord. Ye risk war to get out of marrying Acair."

Meredith gasped, how dare he? Pressing her lips together, she glared at her guard. "Ye should take care, Angus. One could consider yer words as–"

Her guard raised a hand. "Dona questions my loyalty, my lady. I serve ye as loyally as I do yer father. But as yer father isna here, I feel I must speak on his behalf. Whatever yer thoughts, yer feelings, consider the consequences. War is never pretty."

"Really? Ye forget if I marry Acair it willna be war that finishes us off." Meredith shifted in the saddle, her fingers tugging at the reins. Beneath her, her mount tossed his head, eager to be off. Her guard's words had weight, but she couldna turn from the future of her clan if it meant sacrificing one for the many. The threat was far too great. "Nay, Angus, 'tisna war I risk. Ye know as well as I, war is as much a way of life as the rain and wind. The clans have been feuding for generations. A war with the Sinclair clan or any clan we could win. It is not the Highlanders we must fear - what do ye think will become of us if the English get hold of our lands? Is it not enough that they already control the lowlands? If there was hope Sinclair would turn from an alliance with England, I would do my duty as a good daughter should, but we both know his interest is only in securing an alliance with England and seizing power. His son is no better, greedy, cruel. It is not a fate I would wish upon anyone - not even an Englishwoman."

"I have said my piece, my lady. I pray ye ken what will happen."

"Put your mind at ease. I know what it is I do. Dona forget, Oich Creek. Bring Lindsay, and if he resists, ye will do what is necessary."

"Do ye know where Oich Creek is? It's a good day's hard ride from here. Baird will ride with ye and then he will seek out a priest." Angus shook his head. "There are those with less than honourable intentions. Either a guard goes with ye or ye stay here. I willna be swayed, my lady. The entire plot doesna settle well with me."

Time wasna a friend. The longer they debated, the harder it would all be. Meredith exhaled sharply. "As ye wish, I will take Baird with me, ye see to the rest of my command being carried out. Keep in mind, Angus, the fate of our people rests upon our success with this ruse."

"Aye, as ye command, Lady Meredith." Angus whirled on one heel and strode away.

Baird appeared at her side, a frown twisting his features. "If ye intend to reach the farmstead, 'tis best we leave now. A storm brews to the east and this early in the year there may yet be snow within the clouds."

"Aye, we ride. Pray, Baird, our plot bears fruit," Meredith shuddered and nudged her mount forward. The wind's cold fingers danced across her skin, and she tugged her brat higher.

Please, God, let her sway Ailen and see her kin to freedom.

~*~

Icy clumps of snow and debris clung to the edge of the creek as Meredith guided her horse into the slow-moving water. Small flakes drifted on the wind, swirling and dancing in the air.

"Lady Meredith, we need to turn south." Concern dripped from Baird's voice and she glanced over her shoulder.

"There is little time–"

"My lady, we ride along the border of Lindsey territory. If we are caught, there will be hell to pay." Baird gestured to a rocky outcropping along the edge of a hill. "As far as they know, ye are the daughter of their enemy and a fair prize. If they see ye–"

Her stomach dropped. Baird's words sank into her mind. Indeed, the clan knew nothing of the arrangement. If they were to be caught…nay, she couldna be concerned with such things. Haste was needed and any extra delay could ruin the tenuous agreement. "'Tis a risk we must take, Baird. It cuts nearly a half day from our journey. Angus may already be on his way."

"Then we must make haste. The Lindsey's would be only too happy to seize ye. Their chieftain willna have had time to let his men know of yer agreement."

If Ailen had made it back to the gathering. So many things could go wrong. Meredith blinked, her eyes burning. God help them if she failed. How she wished she knew if Angus had intercepted Ailen by now.

Memories of Ailen flitted through her mind. Her skin prickled where he had touched her. A gentle touch, but one filled with strength. Thousand wings beat within her belly. She pressed her lips together to halt the smile tugging at them.

Bloody hell, Meredith shook her head. She had no time for such thoughts.

"We will take the utmost care and hurry. I wouldna draw attention."

Baird nodded and adjusted his weight in the saddle. He rested one hand on his sword. "As ye wish, my lady."

Meredith gave a short jery nod and guided her horse forward. They couldna push the animals too hard. It would take longer on foot if the animals fell. Time wasna a friend and the sooner they reached their destination the better.

The gathering storm worsened as they rode. By the time the sun was past the highest point, the ground was white.

It seemed even God laughed and mocked her. Perhaps he favoured the English. The sharp edge of her nail caught between her bottom teeth and she sighed. Noone seemed to ken why she was so repulsed. It wasna only that her betrothed followed his father's shadow as a womanizer and brute…but they sought favour from the English.

It was too horrific to contemplate. Where was their pride, their honour in being Scots?

Proudly Scots, Ailen Lindsey was equally in power to the Sinclairs, but did he offer a better plan? There was safety in becoming his wife for her and those within her clan who couldna defend themselves. Would he truly hold her to his proposal? The question darted across her mind. His offer kept the English at bay and halted Acair in his tracks, but what did it mean for her? "Ye canna be serious. He will take over and ye will be cast aside." Barely audible, Meredith's words were slurred. "The Frazer clan would fall to ruin. Or he will drag ye to his clan."

Powerful, handsome. There was something that stirred a fire within her blood. The flesh along her neck tingled where Ailen's fingers had brushed. A hot trail of sparks danced beneath her skin and settled on her belly. God above, why did she feel such things?

"My lady." Baird's sharp tone cut through her thoughts, and she whipped around to stare at him. He lifted a hand and pointed into the distance.

Meredith focused on where he was pointing. A line of riders rode hard across the step and down into the plain. Hard riding, they number ten as best she could count. Their muted liens fluttered in the wind. There was no doubt the men had spotted her and Baird. It would take no time before they descended upon her and her guard. A hard knot twisting in her throat and her breath caught. Lindsey clan members, if she was to guess.

And choked back a sob. "Lindsey clan members?" Gulping in a deep breath, she looked at her guard, tightening her grip on her mount.

"No doubt, my lady. If we can get through the trees there." Baird nodded toward a stand of trees. "We would be on our land, my lady. Oich Creek and the farmstead are a short gallop beyond the trees."

"Lead on, my friend. I would reach our lands before they intercept us." Meredith pulled her horse's head around and slapped the reins across his flank. The grey bolted toward safety… or as much safety as she could have.

The thunder of the approaching riders echoed in the pounding of her heart. Icy flakes lashed at her face, biting into the tender skin. Leaning forward, she clung to her mount's mane. She had to get to the woods. Meredith risked a glance over her shoulder. Baird galloped a length behind her. Beyond him, the Lindsey men were gaining on them.

"Dona look back, my lady." Baird hollered. "Just go. Go, my lady!"

"I canna leave ye." The wind snatched the words from her throat and Baird waved at her as he pulled his horse to a halt and whirled to face the oncoming men.

"Dona worry about me, dona stop, nor look back, my lady. We are nearly there." The sing of metal on metal filled the air and Meredith's blood froze.

Turning her mount around, Meredith stared at her guard. "Nay, Baird." Her voice cracked. "We are so close. I wouldna leave ye to their intentions."

Her guard glared at her. His horse spun, snorting and tossing its head. "Go. The longer ye linger, the more risk there is. Go." He snarled.

Meredith sobbed and whipped her horse into motion.

God, keep him safe. Please, please, please.

Chapter Seven

Meredith leaned down over her mount's neck, the wind whipping along her skin. Ice and snow flew with each pounding stride of her galloping horse. The thunder of hooves competed with her ragged breathing. A glance behind her revealed no one followed. A small mercy, but the cost was too high.

Biting back a sob, Meredith urged her mount faster.

Sharp and merciless, the branches raked over her face and arms as her horse thrashed through the narrow gaps between the trees. A broken branch slid along her face, scoring the flesh. Pain lanced through her, leaving a cloying taste on her tongue. The tickle of blood trailed down her face to her throat.

Shouting a head preceded shadows moving through the trees in front of her. Her heart dropped and Meredith tightened her grip on the reins. Nay, she couldna fail not when she was so close.

Riders flooded the road in front of her, blocking her path. Meredith yanked on the reins, her mount rearing in protest. She rested a hand on his sweaty neck. "Easy." The soft croon of her voice trembled with emotion.

"'Tis interesting what one can find when one is out hunting." One man nudged his horse closer, his eyes narrowed. "Ye didna think anyone would notice ye on our land?"

"Ye are'na on Lindsey land, ye are Frazer land now and have been for a fair stretch." Meredith straightened in her saddle, tugging on one rein. Beneath her, the horse shifted. A tremble raced along her body as she sucked in a deep breath. "Didna not think anyone would notice ye trespassing?"

The men chuckled, their amusement grating along her nerves. They exchanged looks, jostling each other. Silence stretched around them, painful. The skin along her jaw tightened painfully. Her eyes burned. A strange roaring filled her ears, and she raised a hand to her face. Spots danced at the edge of her vision. "Or did ye not consider ye are'na on yer land? What have ye done with Baird? I hold no illusion ye would—"

"Ye mean the warrior who stood between ye and us?" The apparent leader snickered. "He still draws breath. Our chieftain will decide both of ye's fate."

"Ye are not on yer lands, ye trespass on–"

"She is Sinclair's betrothed. He would pay handsomely to get her back." A voice drifted through the din. "Though, perhaps not as much as her father would."

"I belong to no-one," Meredith ground out through clenched teeth. "Least of all Sinclair or his bastard son. Ye ambushed my guard and I as we travelled. Ye risk war for an imagined slight."

"Nay, my lady. 'Tis not war we risk. Ye Frazer's are'na equal in skill to any of us. In bed with the English - everyone in the highlands knows it. What honour is there amongst ye was erased long ago."

"My kin are fools." Meredith clenched her fists. Good god, when would the error of her lowland kin ever be erased from memory?

She held no love for the English - nor did she hold any love for a fool. "Their error is seeking to keep their position and their lands is their own. Not mine. I hold no loyalty to blampots. Ye would do well to let me pass. Perhaps Chieftain Frazer will forgive such an insult."

"Yer father spends his time worrying about the upcoming nuptials and what they bring to his clan." Hot breath washed over the back of her neck and Meredith whirled. An older warrior with greying hair and a full beard smirked at her. "His interest in not on a wayward daughter who hasna learned her place."

"We waste time." The man, seemingly in charge, exhaled sharply. "Bind her and let us be on our way. Ailen will be returning from the conference soon and I wouldna–"

Meredith jerked away from the old man's grip and glared at him when he laughed. Another rider appeared on her other side, his leg brushing against hers. He raised a brow and wrapped an arm around her waist, dragging her from the saddle and into his lap.

"Ye waste too much time trying to bend her to yer will, Broderick. She isna more than a woman." He pulled her flush against him and grabbed her wrist. His grip tightened, holding her steady. "Bind her hands so we may be on our way."

Meredith twisted, yanking her wrist from his grasp. "How dare ye? I willna stand for such disregard. Let me go." Dull throbbing in her gut twisted into sharp agonised shards racing along her midsection. Her heart pounded against her ribs. Nay, nay. Please, God, nay. She wouldna be–

"Hold still, woman." Her captor wrapped both arms around her, holding her in a snug grip as the other soldier leaned in and grabbed both wrists. Quick movements and the soldier had a thick rope secured, her hands firmly in front of her. "Be careful, my lady. Ye wouldna want to fall."

Poor Baird. She hadna intended to put him in danger. A simple ruse set on its ear. Meredith blinked to clear the blur from her vision. If only she had taken a moment to consider. The stakes continued to be too high. Her clan, her family, deserved so much more than to be pawns for men driven by greed and lust. Still, she should have considered the cost to those loyal to her. The blood spilled would not easily wash from her hands.

Nay, there wasna point in regrets. These men were eager, loyal - and unaware of the offer she had extended to Ailen.

"She is far prettier than the rumours." The man holding her tightened his grip. "Yet another reason to distrust anything that comes from a Frazer's lips."

"Ye act rashly, Ossigal, and Ailen mayna be so understanding." The leader barked and snagged the reins of Meredith's mount and turned away from the border.

"Aye, a pretty little thing. Perhaps if Ailen has no use for ye, he will see–"

"Ossigal, hold yer tongue."

"She is a prisoner, nothing more."

"She is the daughter of a Chieftain and a woman. Dona forget it." Broderick ground out. "Ye are Scots, not English. Ailen will cut yer heart out if ye dona respect her. Ye know this as well as I." He trotted up, his horse falling into place beside Ossigal's horse, and shot the man holding her a dark look. Broderick reached over, wrapping one arm around her waist, and dragged her onto his mount.

"Ye would do well to remember it yerself." Ossigal snapped and kicked his horse faster.

Her captor snorted but held his tongue. His grip tightened, fingers digging into her side as they moved in unison. The jarring stride of his horse had her backside slapping painfully against the hard leather of the saddle. She clung to the horse's mane, unwilling to lean back against him. Meredith bit back a cry. She wouldna give him the satisfaction of voicing a complaint.

Dark clouds continued to gather overhead as they kept a steady pace through the thick brush. Branches caught on the edge of her brat, tangling in her hair. A sharp branch raked across her face, leaving a stinging trail in its wake.

A heavy grey cloak clung to the day. The chill soaked through her brat and liene, sinking into her bones. Shivering, her teeth chattering wildly, Meredith hunched in on herself, icy tendrils of moisture dripping down her back.

The group left the trees, a wide open sea of brown swayed in the breeze. Ice and snow clung to the ground, shrouded in shadow. "Ye are about to shake yerself from my horse." Broderick wrapped the end of his brat around her. "Ailen will see me to an early grave if ye take to yer death bed with a chill."

Meredith looked at him from the corner of her eye. "I am not so weak." She lifted her bound hands to wipe the damp hair from her face. "But thank ye for yer kindness."

Broderick shrugged in response and guided his mount around a large boulder, the movement nearly unseating her. "The farmstead is just up the glen. We will await Ailen there."

Meredith straightened. Were they really so close, within shouting distance? She scanned the far edge of the field, her heart in her throat. Through the haze of the snow and sleet, she could make out the hulk of a building and offered a quick prayer of thanks.

A simple cottage, the grey stone of the walls held up a thatched roof. The building stood sentry, the darkened windows peering out like a warrior's eyes. Seeing all but giving nothing away.

Meredith shuddered. A chill reached through to wrap itself around her soul and squeeze. In spite of herself, she could feel the faint tinge of fear fading. She was a captive, aye, but among these men there was none of the terror.

If she were in the hands of Sinclair warriors, her fate would be far different. The realisation clawed its way down her spine. Despite being their enemy, the men had treated her with dignity…so far.

Dear god what had she gotten herself into?

~*~

Ailen guided his horse through the dense brush, the branches scratching along his thighs. Meredith's offer played at the edge of his memory and he toyed with the edge of his reins. They were close to the farmstead - his farmstead.

Mathieus Frazer would honour his daughter's arrangement and he would claim the land as his own. Just as he would claim Meredith.

At the edge of the treeline Ailen halted and peered across the field at the small cottage. Smoke curled upward from the chimney, a faint light flickered in the windows. Tethered beyond the house, a handful of horses grazed. Figures moved at the edge of the cottage, a guard.

"Yer men already await ye." Angus nudged his horse forward, bumping into Ailen's. "Pray they have'na laid a hand upon–"

"Ye need not worry." Ailen shifted in his saddle. His men were nothing if not honourable. To them, she was a prize worthy of him, and him alone. They wouldna touch her. "My men wouldna dare insult me by harming a woman. No matter who she was, they would know the price of my displeasure. Meredith is safe. The kitten thinks herself a wolf." He chuckled.

"Ye will find she is more wolf than pup. Meredith thinks herself a warrior."

"Meredith has been heir to our clan since she was a little girl." The branches parted and Baird rode out. "From the moment her mother and brother died, she has become daughter and son."

"Heir or no, she is a woman. One yer beloved chieftain would deliver to Sinclair." Ailen shot the pair a dark glance. He held little love for the current chieftain of the Sinclair clan, a weak, bitter excuse for a man. Knowing the Sinclairs had ambushed a Lindsey family only added to his hatred.

"Sinclair seeks to gain favour with Edward. Mathieus knows it isna the optimal match, but there is little he can do. Lady Meredith is a handful and our chieftain is aware few would look at her twice. More than one man has told her father he needs to take her in hand." Angus grunted. "Lady Meredith offers ye a bounty, and a chance to humiliate the bastards."

"Aye, she does. It does leave me with questions, though." Ailen shifted in his saddle, half twisting to stare at the two warriors flanking him. "Did ye tell her the truth, lads? Hmm? Baird, does yer Lady know about yer ties to the Lindsay clan?" He snorted when the two men shared a glance, their faces darkening though with shame or the cold he couldna say. "I dona think she would be too pleased to know ye are considered kin."

"Lady Meredith is a fine lady, one too good for the likes of that animal. I dona believe she needs to know of my family's ties to anyone beyond our clan." Baird shifted, the grey light falling upon the dark purple mark across his face. His lip split, blood crusted along the edge of the wound.

"Enough talk." Scowling, Angus waved a hand forward. "There is much to be discussed and Lady Meredith deserves to be present. She will worry herself into a mood until she knows we are safe."

"Aye, she will." Baird ducked his head, his shoulders hunched.

Ailen cast a glance over to the two men. Damn. It was a fine mess he found himself in, but one he refused to step away from. He would honour his word and Meredith Frazer would marry him. In doing so, she would yield her ties to her clan to him and he would shore up the weakness within the highland Frazers until they could stand on their own. Her reaction to the truth of her guards, however, left him at odds. Would she resent her men for their deceit?

Meredith was unlike anything he could have pictured. The rumours held naught but a grain of truth to them. There was such fire within her, and his fingers burned to touch her. The skin where her hair had caressed him tingled at the memory playing in his head. Meredith needed a strong man, one who understood she wasna weak or easily controlled. One who would tame her - not break her.

"In truth, it is time she put aside the foolishness of her youth. She is the daughter of our—"

"Meredith is mine." Ailen's hard tone cut across the space between them and he met both men's stares. "From the moment ye put yer faith in her plot and chose me. Insult her and ye insult me."

"I meant no insult, sir," Baird choked out. "I speak only the truth. Too long has she been permitted to run wild? She needs a firm hand. It is not a flaw I speak of."

Ailen grunted and kicked his horse into a canter, heading across the field. Angus and Baird followed him. The anger simmering beneath the surface had almost eased. Two men to guard a treasure such as Meredith? Aye, he couldna fault their loyalty - their common sense, however.

No matter. Meredith was his - by her own plotting.

Halfway across the field, he caught a movement from around the house and smirked. So his men werena sleeping. Good. Pushing his horse harder, Ailen crossed the field and pulled up by the west wall of the house.

"Chieftain." Brodrick stepped from beneath the overhang. "We didna expect ye so soon. What of them?" He jerked his chin toward Angus and Baird.

"Ye know well they are Lady Meredith's guard."

"Thought we were free of the likes of ye," Brodrick sneered, stepping into the path of Baird and Angus's horses. "Pity I was wrong."

"If yer werena married to my cousin, ye wouldna be of this world." Baird nudged his horse forward, forcing Brodrick back a step. "How does Lady Meredith fare?"

Brodrick jumped back, glowering at him. "My wife used to be yer cousin. A fact I try not to dwell on too much."

The familiar bickering grated across Ailen's nerves. Until the matter with Meredith was settled, they were trespassers on Frazer's land. And while he had no issue with knocking a bit of sense into the Frazer warriors, it didna look good when they were to become allies. "Enough. There are far more important things to consider. What of a priest?" Ailen dismounted, tossing the reins at Brodrick and stomping around the edge of the house to the front door.

"What need do ye have of a priest?" Broderick shouldered past Angus to fall in step with Ailen. "Her father–"

Ailen shot his soldier a hard glare. "Baird?"

"Father Stephens will join us soon." Baird elbowed Broderick aside. "He was at the gathering with McGreghere and the others."

"Aye, I spoke to him before catching up with ye, Ailen." Angus tugged his brat around his shoulders. "He left shortly after Lady Meredith with intent to meet us here."

Ailen grunted and reached for the door. He pushed it inward and ducked beneath the beam. Nudging the door closed, Ailen straightened and glanced around. Warmth filled the room, the crackling of wood in the hearth filled the silence. Several candles flickered on the table, casting light across the room. On the narrow bed, curled away from the door, her dark hair cascading across the blankets, Meredith froze.

"This is a bit awkward, would ye not agree?"

Meredith rolled over, eyes wide, and stared at him. She scrambled to her feet; her bound hands pressed to her stomach. Her hair hung down around her face. Several scratch marks covered one cheek, blood crusting along the edges of another along her brow. Tears left pale trails down her face, cutting through the grime.

Ailen clenched his teeth and strode toward her. She backed away with a squeak, tumbling onto the bed. "Nay, nay." The quiver in her voice stroked the embers of his fury, and he grabbed the rope around her wrists and pulled her to her feet.

"We are even, my lady." Ailen reached for the dirk at his waist and sliced through the rope. "One kidnapping deserves another. A fine story to tell our children."

Meredith gaped at him, her eyes wide, a single tear spilling down her face. He reached up and wiped the tear from her cheek. "I didna have a chance to tell my men of our arrangement." He nudged her toward the table. "Sit, I am certain the men have found something to eat. The priest will be here shortly."

Chapter Eight

Meredith rubbed at the raw skin on her wrists and stared at the man in front of her. Her stomach fluttered and rolled. Leg's braced apart, hands behind his back, Ailen stood a few steps away. Despite his words, there was none of the sheer terror that filled her at the thought of marrying Acair.

"Meredith?"

Had she gone daft? Surely he hadn't said what she thought she had heard. "Priest?" Baird was to get the priest only after they'd arrived. Only Baird was on the trail, probably dead or worse.

"Aye," Ailen stepped closer until the hard length of his body was pressed against her. A shiver raced along her body with the hot wash of his breath against her ear. "Ye didna forget my terms, did ye, my lady?"

She hadna forgotten, instead she had prayed she could convince him to put aside his terms and just take the land. Nay, it was a falsehood; she told herself. By her own hand, she had consented to his terms and she couldna go back now.

There were too many pieces in play, too much to go wrong. Meredith lifted one hand and bit down on the tip of her thumb. Good god, was she ready to become a bride? A wife? The plan to halt her marriage…

What of love? What of the marriage she imagined her mother and father had? Her desire to have a husband who wanted her - the woman, not the heir?

Such childish thoughts didna belong to a woman, they belonged to a girl. Marriage wasna game to be played. Wasna her intent to save them from Sinclair's influence and being overrun by the English?

Her pride and longing for foolish things was a minor thing compared to their wellbeing. Meredith chewed at the edge of her nail, her teeth cutting through it. Aye, Ailen was a man of his word. She eyed him from through her lashes. A muscle ticked in his jaw, the only outward indication of his emotions. He didna press her to rush.

"My lord, 'tis only fair, I remind ye. My intent is to—"

"Ye have my word, Meredith." Ailen offered a small smile, the lines around his eyes deepening. "The last thing I will ever do is side with the English. Sinclair and his lust for them is a blight upon the highlands."

His words cut through the weight in her stomach, and the lump unravelled. Her heart stuttered in her chest and she swallowed. At least he wouldna negotiate with the enemy.

"Ye will become my wife, lady of my clan. Yer clan will be strengthened by the union and Sinclair and his bastard son will fall."

"If ye be certain, ye wish to marry me." Meredith pressed her fingers to her lips and straightened her shoulders. "It isna required. The events of our meeting thus far can be overlooked."

"Nay, Lady Meredith." Ailen shook his head and reach up to wrap a lock of her hair through his fingers. "Ye offer me two hundred trained men, not boys. Land. Salt. A bounty far too to rich for a simple ruse. I will ensure Acair Sinclair doesna become yer husband."

"And what would ye have of me?"

Ailen chuckled, his gaze trailing over her features, heat flaring in the depths of his brown eyes. "What every wife offers her husband." He grasped her chin between his fingers and thumb, the heat of his touch searing into her skin and setting her blood on fire. "Ye will be my wife, Meredith. A Lindsey not a Frazer. Ye will sit by my side through feast and famine. And ye will provide me with heirs."

Her cheeks burning, Meredith shifted in his grip. Her body was on board with such a plan, though her heart ached for what he didna offer. "What if–" A shadow beyond the small window moved and her mind darted in the direction of the men she'd ridden with. What had become of Baird and Angus? Were they still alive? God above, she had forgotten her own guard.

"Ye know my conditions, Meredith."

"Ye will tell me what became of my guard." She grabbed his hand and clung to it. Warm and calloused, his hands all but engulfed hers. Ailen squeezed gently, his fingers curling around hers. Pressing their joined hands to her chest, she licked her lips. "They were–"

Ailen tilted his head slightly, a slow smirk curling his lips. "Ah, it seems there is much still to be discussed. Yer men are safe. They shall remain at yer side even after we are wed."

"Ye would trust them?" Meredith sucked in a quick breath and lowered her head to press their hands to her forehead. "Aye, ye are'na like some. A man's worth is in his loyalty until he becomes disloyal, then he is dealt with swiftly. I remember my father saying that is how ye deal with men. I sought only to save my people from a horrid fate. Their well being must come before the consideration of one."

"There are other–"

"Nay," Meredith loosened her grip, only to have him take both her hands and tug her closer. He wrapped one arm around her waist, holding her captive, the other a hot weight against her neck. She shivered, heat washing through her from her head to her toes. "There are no other options, my lord. My father is still strong. Old, but by no means weak. He will mourn my choice for a moment, then will rejoice, I am certain."

She straightened her shoulders and raised her chin. Her head bumping into his chin. Leaning back as far as his embrace would allow, Meredith met his gaze. "So be it. Though I dona think there is a priest yet arrived."

"He was summoned and will be here soon."

Meredith nodded, a strange calm settling over her shoulders. As if she were watching rather than taking part, Meredith bowed her head to the man who would be her husband. "If it would please ye, I would like a chance to wash. I wouldna tell my father or my bairns that I married with mud and blood upon my face and my hair tangled with branches. Then, if he is here, we will set in motion our arrangement."

"Aye, Meredith, ye will have a wash. I will see if the priest has arrived and if the men's hunt was successful. I'll send in water for ye to wash with." Ailen brushed a thumb over her cheek. "It will be no grand celebration, but ye will be wed today." He brushed a soft kiss along her lips and stepped back.

Meredith licked her tingling lips and gaped at him. Had he - he had. Goodness, she swallowed her gazed darting to his lips before she ducked her head. Ailen's soft chuckle drew her ire, and she met his stare.

Flames danced in his eyes as he painted a path over her features with his gaze, settling on her lips. His tongue darted out, lingering along the edge of his mouth for a second before sweeping her closer. Her breasts crushed against his chest, Meredith had a moment to suck in a quick breath. Ailen's mouth descended on hers. It was hard, demanding. His tongue sank into her mouth, stroking and caressing, teasing her tongue to dance with his.

His hands caressed her back, stroking along the delicate line of her spine. Sparks flared to life beneath his touch, and she whimpered. A yawning, yearning pit formed in her stomach and she clung to him. She pressed closer, her knees buckling.

Ailen pulled away, dropping one more quick kiss to her lips. "Ah, Meredith, my lass, ye will be the death of me yet." He released her, the slow slide of his hands along her body leaving burning trails in their wake. With a final look, he turned on one heel and strode from the room.

The floor beneath her feet trembled with each stride he took and the slamming of the door brought a cascade of dust raining down over her. She stumbled back, bumping into the table. Resting one hand on the rough wooden surface, she stared at the door, her heart in her throat.

What is god's name had she gotten herself into?

~*~

Meredith tucked the last lock of her hair behind one ear and adjusted her brat. Male voices bantered back and forth beyond the door and a quick look revealed the snow had picked up again. Fat flakes drifted down in the fading light, obscuring the trees a short distance from the window.

"Lady Meredith?" Unfamiliar and crackling, the male voice preceded a short knock and the door swinging inward.

She took a deep breath and faced the door where a tall, lean man with greying hair hovered, one hand on the door. The long black robes he wore spoke of his position, and she felt her stomach jump.

"Aye?"

"I'm Father Stevens." He stepped inside and nudged the door closed, though not all the way. "'Tis a blustery day for a wedding, my child."

"What is a bit of snow? Spring is here, it will melt." Meredith smothered her skirts and clasped her hands together. "As all seasons do."

"I must ask, Lady Meredith, are ye wanting this union?"

Meredith flexed her fingers before tucking her hands behind her. Wanting? Nay, needing. "Father, ye need not worry about me. I have no doubts Ailen Lindsey is a man of honor."

The priest chuckled and shuffled a little closer. Concern darkened his grey eyes, and he stared at her. "He is a good man. But ye didna answer my question. If ye not be wanting the union–"

Meredith held up her right hand and shook her head. The time for such thoughts had long since passed. She had secured her fate the moment Ailen had ridden from her presence back in Corich. "I will wed Ailen today, Father Stevens. Ailen will be my husband and 'tis a choice and decision I have made, sir."

"What of yer father? Chieftain Frazer mayna be so eager to approve. There isna anyone who doesna understand ye are to wed Acair Sinclair."

"My father knows I wouldna marry Sinclair. We have spoken at length. Nay, while the manner is unique, Father Stevens, my chieftain and father will understand. He knows me only too well." Meredith clapped her hands and forced a smile to her lips. "So, shall we get on with it? The hour draws late and I dona think ye wish to sleep upon the ground tonight."

"Nay, I do prefer a warm bed to the cold ground. Already there is fresh snow gathered, and it is a rather uncomfortable resting place. Very well. Come, I shall escort ye out to yer husband." He offered his arm with a gentle smile.

Meredith resisted the urge to chew her nail and reached out. The rough material of his robe brushed against her fingertips and she bit back a shaky breath. Her future was set and there would be no going back. Her vision blurred, eyes burning, she blinked and peeked out the narrow strip of the open door. Ailen, flanked by two of his soldiers, waited, facing the door.

She didna want to retreat. The man she had chosen was a good one. Nay, it was time. Each step measured, she kept her attention on the movement of her feet. By the end of the day, she would be a wife - and quite possibly the cause of a war in the highlands.

Chapter Nine

Meredith adjusted her brat around her shoulders, the material little defence against the growing unrest within her heart. She was wed. A wife in name - but there was little doubt she would be his before the night was done.

She swept the interior of the cottage with a cursory glance. The scarred table and chairs took up most of the room. However, it was what lay within the shadows of the flames from the hearth that drew her focus.

A thick wooden frame held what would be her bed. Simple sheets covered the mattress, along with several thick furs and woollen blankets. Ailen's thick brat had been rolled up and lay across the head of the bed.

"Yer pride is of little concern, Meredith." She crept across the room, guided by an invisible hand. She reached out with a trembling hand and ran her fingers over the furs. "Ye are married now. Yer duty is to yer husband and his clan. The safety and well being of yer people are worth any cost."

"Who do ye speak to?" Ailen's voice rumbled through the room and she whirled to gape at him.

"No one, Chieftain." Meredith offered a one shoulder shrug and clenched her hands together. The urge to chew on her thumbnail almost more than she could bear. Her heart flipped in her chest and she swayed on her feet. Bracing herself against the edge of the bed, she forced herself to stand still.

"What do ye think will happen tonight?"

Heat rolled up her throat to stain her cheeks. She really had no idea. There had been no time to dwell on such things at home. The household had always needed something. From the whispers she had overheard, she knew it was not necessarily a pleasant task, but it needed to be done. She had given her word. If only she had spent a little time question the married women - but she had given little thought to what happened between a man and a woman. "I didna consider ye wouldna have just accepted our soldiers."

Ailen laughed softly as he approached. He reached out, grabbing her hands and tugging her closer. "Aye, ye were prepared to barter for the safety for yer people, no matter the cost."

Her body trembled, and she tugged on her hands. Goodness, he didna need to hold her captive. Her word was her oath, and she had agreed to their union. She would do her duty - no matter how painful or awkward.

"I would have it over with." Meredith sucked in a quick breath. "Ye have my vow. I willna go back on my word, Ailen… I mean Chieftain Lindsey." She pulled her hands free and twisted away. "Let us see to the issue at hand and be done with it."

Ailen wrapped a hand around her wrist, his touch burning through her courage as he tugged her back against his body. "Ah, so eager. A fine trait for a wife. No man wishes to be considered a chore."

Meredith fidgeted, his words searing through her defences, to settle like hot ash along her heart. "I wouldna know about such things." Swallowing around the lump in her throat, she leaned to the side, putting a tiny bit of distance between them.

He chuckled and tightened his grip around her waist. The hot wash of his breath against her neck sent waves of tingles along her body, and she shivered. She shifted, the drag of the fabric of her liene against her nipples almost painful. "The hour grows late, and if we are to leave early in the morning, perhaps we should retire for the night. I am not–"

"Nay, I dona think ye would know." Ailen trailed his lips along the curve of her shoulder. "Ah, there is a certain pride a man takes when he knows his wife wants him. Is willing to take him between her thighs. There is nothing quite like the soft silk of a woman's skin, wife."

Meredith ducked her head. She coughed, hoping to dislodge the lump in her throat, and turned her head slightly so she could peek at him from the corner of her eye. "It is my duty to give ye what ye want, what ye need. A wife should always take care of her husband."

Ailen's grip tightened, his fingers digging into her waist before he spun her around to face him. He wrapped his calloused hands around her face, holding her gaze with his. "Duty is a poor bedmate, Meredith. In truth, to be ruled by it is to find oneself cold and empty. I willna have a shell in my bed." He reached up, tangling his fist in her hair and tugged her head back. "Ye are no wilting flower, Meredith. Ye have shown me it otherwise. Nay, if ye were the wilting, dutiful woman, ye would have me believe ye wouldna ambushed me with yer proposal - nor would ye have agreed to my offer. Ye would have waited for Acair to appear and wed him."

"Ye canna know that."

"I can know it. I will have all of ye. Do ye ken?"

A weak whimper escaped, and she nodded. She licked her lips, her mouth dry, her pulse skittering beneath the cage of her skin. "One for the many." Meredith murmured, her stare darting around. She exhaled a shaky breath and looked him in the eyes. ""Tis dangerous what you speak, Ailen. I admit I yearn for more, but ye dona ken what will happen."

"Nay, Meredith," Ailen trailed the backs of his fingers down her face, over her jaw, and swept over her collarbone. "I ken exactly what is to happen. Ye are my wife. Yer kin are tied to mine by that alliance. Put all thoughts of kin and home from yer mind, wife. Tonight, we will learn about each other before we are forced back to our duties."

Meredith cleared her throat, unable to catch her breath.

Her lips parted, soft puffs of air passing through them as she stared at him. Tingling danced along her body, as if a thousand butterflies caressed her body. "Ye speak so sweetly of things. I mayna have a true understanding, but I—"

Ailen pressed his finger to her lips and leaned closer. His hot breath ghosted over her bare skin. It burned through her nerves, her body leaning toward him. "I know no more than ye, Meredith." He trailed his lips over her forehead, pressing soft, moist kisses along her nose, her cheeks. "Tonight, we shall learn together." Ailen tilted her chin upward, his lips descending over hers.

He licked along the seam of her lips, pressure on her chin forcing her mouth open. She whimpered, grabbing hold of his arms as he plundered her mouth. Flames leapt within her body, her blood boiling through her veins.

Her breath quickened. His lips were warm, dry. The faint tickle of his beard teased the tender skin around her lips. She gasped, and he took control, his tongue sweeping into her mouth and plundering with ruthless need.

He traced the contours of her mouth, his tongue stroking along hers, giving and taking. Meredith clung to him. Her moan of desire sliced through the silence and pulled her flush against him. The thin material of her liene grated across her nipples. Heat pooled between her legs, her pussy aflame. God, but he knew how to kiss.

The distinct flavour of Ailen flooded her tongue. Meredith closed her eyes, soaking into the rolling waves crashing over her. The world spun around her and she dug her fingers into his shoulders, moving closer.

He slid his hands down her body, fingers dancing across every curve. She shivered, sparks exploding where he touched bare skin. Ailen nipped at her bottom lip, the sharp sting soothed by a slow lave of his tongue across the tender skin. Meredith shifted, her knees threatening to give out.

"Ailen." Moaning his name, Meredith shifted against him. Her body on fire, She pressed closer to Ailen. A hollow ache settled over her. Made clumsy with desire, she pulled at the collar of his lien, her fingertips raking over bare skin. Like a starving woman, she needed more. Needed something, anything, to ease the ache between her thighs.

Ailen growled, a low, animalistic sound as he crushed her within his arms. He shuffled backwards, stopping when the edge of their bed hit the back of his legs. Using his weight, he bore her onto the bed, never stopping his exploration of her neck with his lips.

He trailed his hand down her shoulder. Bunching the material of her liene in his as he nibbled and licked along the bared flesh. With each touch of his lips, Meredith's ragged breathing echoed like thunder in her ears. Roughened by war and hard work, his calloused skin seduced her nerve endings, leaving burning paths of heat and embers over her tender skin. Over the curve of her breast, along the dip of her waist, to her hip, he stopped only long enough to loosen the ties on her liene and push it off her shoulders. "Ah, Meredith, ye will be the death of me." Gutteral, his voice struck a chord within her body and she shuddered.

"Ailen, please."

Slipping his fingers beneath the thin fabric, he traced the warm skin beneath." Shh, wife, I'll see to yer needs, and my own." He crushed her mouth beneath his, sweeping his tongue inside and claiming her. The world spun around her with each glide of his tongue against hers. His breath caressed her face. Breaking from her lips, he rained soft, biting kisses along her jaw and down her throat.

"Should be outlawed to hide such beauty beneath yer clothing." Ailen pushed at her liene, sliding it over one shoulder. The neckline caught on one nipple, hanging there as if tempting him to act.

His beard pricked and prodded the embers in her blood, scraping across her throat and jaw. Ailen licked along the exposed skin until he got to the curve of her breast. He nuzzled against the flesh, pushing the fabric aside and taking her erect nipple between his lips. Hot, empty, a deep yearning throbbed between her thighs. Moisture gathered, and she squeezed her legs together to ease the burning beneath the damp curls.

Shards of pleasure spread through her like arrows, and she cried out.

Ailen groaned and licked and suckled at the dip in her throat. His free hand tangled in her hair, tugging on the dark strands.

Meredith clutched at his shoulders with trembling hands. It shouldna feel so good. God, above, she was on fire.

A deep yearning throbbed between her legs. Hot, wet, her body cried out for something she didna know. Her breathing caught in her throat and she bit back a whimper.

Every nerve ending in her body danced within the flames. She swayed against him, her fingers digging into his arms. Waves of pleasure rolled over her, the faint thread of fear beneath them fading with each slow caress.

Ailen trailed his hand across her throat and down. His rough, calloused skin burned a path, his blunt nails scratching along the curve of her breasts. Each ragged breath brushed her hard nipples against the tip of his thumb. He tugged at the thin fabric of her leine, baring her to his gaze and his touch.

Meredith tipped her head back and closed her eyes.

Ailen's breath scalded her skin, his teeth branded her. She shuddered at the first brush of his thumb over one nipple. "Ailen."

"So sweet," Ailen pushed the last, stubborn bit of cloth to the ground and bent his knees. He wrapped both arms around her legs, just under buttocks and lifted her. Swinging her around, Ailen laid her out across the furs, slotting his hips between her thighs.

Meredith gasped and clung to him. Ailen ran a hand down her hip, wrapping his fingers around her thigh. Each digit dug into the tender skin as he lifted her leg over his forearm. The covers beneath them bunched beneath her hips, his hand tangling within them.

Her heel bumped against the curve of his ass, and she whimpered. "Ailen." Fear wove through her tone and he hushed her with a soft sound.

Ailen shifted, the hard press of his erection poking at the soft curls protecting her womanhood. Bracing himself over her with one hand pressed against the bed by her head, Ailen locked gazes with her. "Ah, a true gift. A vision for the eyes." Ailen licked his lips. "I wonder if ye taste as sweet as ye look?"

Her cheeks burning, Meredith swallowed and reached above her, her fingers digging into the bedding. She tugged on it, attempting to pull it down over her face. She arched her hips off the bed, her body

"Nay, I would see ye," Ailen commanded. He pressed her deeper into the bed and reached down to wrap both hands around her thighs. The move pushed her legs apart, exposing her core.

Holding her gaze, Ailen bit down on the soft flesh of her belly before he moved downward. He licked along her folds, drawing them into his mouth and rolling them on his tongue.

Meredith hissed a startled breath and wriggled against his grip. The need to flee at odds with the inferno raging within her body. Squeezing her eyes shut, Meredith found herself adrift in a raging sea of sensations.

Waves of pleasure rolled over her from where Ailen lay between her thighs. He worshipped her, lapping and sucking at her folds. Meredith writhed beneath his ministrations, choking back sobs and cries.

She locked her fingers on the covers, her body buffeted to and fro by Ailen's touch. When she feared she couldna stand another second, he drew his tongue along her folds, flicked over the hard, numb hidden, shifted over her.

"Open yer eyes, Meredith." Ailen's ragged voice held a note of command, one she couldna disobey.

She blinked her at him. The gold of his whiskers glistened with moisture, lips swollen, eyes darkened. He looked wrecked in the most primal of manners. He held her gaze as he crawled up her body, the slow drag of his flesh sliding against hers drawing a whimper.

Only when he hovered over her, face to face, did he shift. Reaching between their bodies, he guided his hard cock to her opening and slid inside. Inch by inch, stretching and filling. He toyed with her clit, sending bolts of pleasure thundering through her.

Meredith gasped and arched into his touch. The movement forced him deep within her, and she groaned softly.

Ailen growled, a low, rumbling sound, and rested his hand on her hip. "Give me but a moment, woman. Oh God, ye are so hot, so tight. Makes a man glad to be one." He rolled his hips, easing the rest of the way in.

Meredith bit her lip, her fists tightening around the blankets. "Apolo–"

"Nay, dona apologise Meredith," Ailen chuckled, a rough sound with little mirth. "'Tis not a flaw I speak of."

"Should it not hurt?" Meredith's soft whisper echoed within her head and she stared up at her husband. "I thought–"

"So naïve, so innocent." Ailen chuckled. "Or ye were at least."

Ailen ducked his head, sucking and biting at her lips until she granted him access. He swept inside, stroking along her tongue. He licked along the roof of her mouth, the harsh panting of his breath filling her ears.

"Meredith, lass." Ailen grunted and rolled his hips. Bracing himself on his forearms, he ran his fingers through her hair and began to move. With each thrust of his hips, the pleasure built.

It coiled tighter in her loins. Heat rose along her neck and into her cheeks, a familiar sensation gathering between her legs. Oh god, nay, she couldna need…nay. Nay. Meredith gasped and pushed against his shoulders. She bucked her hips, her body at war with itself until the coil exploded, sending her into a quivering sea of pleasure. Every inch of her body hummed between her legs, throbbed and clamped down around his hard shaft.

Ailen grunted, his thrusts growing harder, rougher. With a final thrust, Ailen hovered over her, his arms quivering. "God above lass."

"Didna I please–"

"Ye would have killed me if ye pleased me anymore." Ailen pressed a hard kiss to her lips. He rolled, wrapping an arm around her shoulders, and used his other hand to cup her ass and hold her against him.

Meredith wiggled in protest and pushed against his chest. Ailen clamped down, wrapping his legs around hers and locking her in place. He tucked her head under her chin and tugged the covers up over her.

His softening cock slid from her body, and she gasped. How could he think of her to be so?–

"Sleep, wife. Tomorrow will be a long day." Ailen yawned and stretched beneath her. "Made worse by how sore ye may be. Sleep, Meredith. Ye are safe."

"I wouldna wish to impose upon ye. Perhaps I can–"

"Ye are mine, Meredith. There is no imposition. Now, sleep." He slapped her backside, the sharp crack of sound loud in the silence. She jumped, the brief flare of pain fading beneath his palm.

What had she done?

~*~

Ailen leaned against the wall of the cottage, his gaze locked on the sleeping woman across the room. Meredith curled under the combined weight of their brats, her hair spilling across the pillow and over one arm. The flicking of the fire cast a golden glow across the expanse of bare skin on display. He shifted, the low curl of desire flickering to life within his belly.

The softness of her skin teased along his memory, the taste of her on his lips enough to taunt his control. Two days they'd spent within the confines of the cottage while the snow gathered. Hours spent in silence and in passion.

They couldna delay further. His clan was at war and there would be little time for more than the responsibilities and duties of his station. Though, in truth, having a new wife lessened his desire for such things.

Meredith sighed and rolled over in her sleep, her covers slipping to reveal the curve of a pale, freckled shoulder. His wife. A woman of passion and fire. His blood heated, and a familiar tingle settled in his groin. Aye, he could see why Sinclair would want her. And why he would never have her? Meredith was his now - and by God, any who dared to challenge the truth would suffer his wrath.

Soft rapping at the door had him straightening with a curse. Ailen stalked across the room and ripped the door open. Angus stood flanked by Broderick and Ossigal.

"What is it?"

"Frazer warriors approach from the north." Angus gestured toward the far edge of the clearing. "Most likely Mathieus has realised Meredith isna simply keeping busy with her usual duties."

"They would be easily defeated. Little more than children, ill-equipped for the weather or war." Borderick grunted, a scowl darkening his features. "There are ten of them."

Angus straightened and shoved the younger man aside. "Young but not unskilled. They are Lady Meredith's kin, able-bodied and, as far as they know, ye are'na to be here." His voice dripped with an icy fury. "'Tis likely they look for Lady Meredith only, as she is known to ride out when upset."

Ailen glared at Broderick. The damn fool would go to war with his own shadow. "They are kin, bound by marriage, and by alliance. Even knowing this ye would slaughter them? May God grant us all a reprieve if ye ever take control of yer own clan. Ye will see 'em all to an early grave." Ailen ground out with a shake of his head. He turned to the other two men. "Meredith's kin are not to be cut down. Meredith and I are wed. She is my wife, and these lands are now mine."

"Aye, they belong to the Lindsey–"

"Me." Ailen's soft-spoken word cut through Broderick's bluster and he met the other man's stare. "Dona forget, with our union, what is hers becomes mine. Gather the men and alert them to the incoming riders. Should temper rise, we hold the benefit of Meredith to speak for us."

"A woman speaks for us now," Ossigal grunted, lips pressed together in a firm line, eyes narrowed, a darkness in his eyes. "Almost as unheard of as an honest Englishman."

"Ossigal."

"She is yer wife and I am loyal to her as such - dona mean I have to like it." Ossigal turned and stomped away.

Ailen exhaled and looked between Broderick and Angus. "I trust the two of ye can prevent bloodshed."

"It will be done. Chieftain Lindsey, ye must know ye can'na remain here. If Mathieus knows if yer presence, ye can be certain Sinclair will learn of it soon. As much as I would like to kill me a few of the bastards, I wouldna have Lady Meredith see such a sight."

"Agreed." Ailen half turned and looked over his shoulder. There was no indication Meredith had awakened. A small blessing for the moment. "We will depart as soon as I have dealt with the Frazer soldiers. There is much to be done, and I would return to my home without delay."

"And yer wife?"

"Lady Meredith isna some wilting flower," Angus elbowed Broderick, forcing the other man to stumble away. "She will be prepared."

"She's a Frazer—"

"Meredith is a Lindsey, and my wife, Broderick." Ailen allowed a small smirk to cross his face. "She is made of sterner, stronger stuff than any Frazer. Meredith will do what is needed, just as we will. See to it, we are ready to ride as soon as the Frazer soldiers have departed."

"And what if ye, my lord?"

Ailen eyed Broderick for a moment. The brashness of the young soldier was not a flaw. Broderick's challenges and questions were welcomed to a point. In time, the young man would learn there were risks that all leaders faced. "I will ensure Meredith is ready to ride. Angus, ye will see to her mount. I willna delay our departure any further."

Angus nodded his head and vanished into the mist around the cabin. Ailen met Broderick's stare for a moment, then turned and stalked back inside. Meredith stirred, tugging their brats up around her and huddling under them. She peers at him through the tangled waves of her hair.

Meredith pushed her hair from her face. "I heard voices."

"Aye, it seems yer father has finally realised ye are absent and sent men to find ye."

Meredith's eyes widened, and she swung her legs over the edge of the bed. She reached for the pale pile of fabric of her liene and pulled it over her head, pushing the brat's aside. "God, 'tis a mess. They willna be swayed–"

"Wife, ye will calm yerself. They have'na arrived yet. I have given my men orders they willna engage with them. No blood will be spilled."

"They willna care yer men willna fight them. They have orders." Meredith tied her liene into place and tugged her brat over her shoulder, securing it with the pin. "They dona know of our arrangement."

"Ye mean our marriage?" Ailen chuckled. "Ye need not worry. Come, ye will greet them by my side." He took her arm and pulled her closer. Wrapping an arm around her shoulder, Ailen guided her out the door and onto the porch. Through the trees, a line of riders galloped, the thunder of hooves growing in the stillness.

The riders crossed the creek, splashing through the water. Young, several were barely old enough to grow a beard. Meredith sucked in a breath and pressed closer to him. "Ye canna hurt them," her voice cracked as she looked at him. "So young. What could Papa be thinking?"

"He isna thinking." Ailen grunted as the riders came to a halt a horse's length away. He straightened, his grip tightening around her waist. "Put yer fears to rest, wife. We dona kill children."

"Lady Meredith." One of the riders bowed his head at Meredith and nudged his mount forward. "Ye are well?"

"Lady Lindsey is quite well." Ailen ground out, the muscle in his jaw ticking beneath his skin. "What brings ye?–"

"Ye are on Frazer land." The soldier glowered at Ailen. "Our Chieftain didna invite ye, yet here ye be."

"Of course," Ailen offered a smile and lifted Meredith's hand to his lips. He brushed his lips over her knuckles and met the soldier's gaze. "'Tis my land - gifted to me by my wife. Lady Meredith's dowry belongs to her husband."

"Ye stole our lady from us." The soldier nudged his horse forward. He focused on Meredith. "Come, my lady, we will see ye home and free of these fools. Chieftain Frazer will be glad to have ye home and safe."

"I am certain Sinclair will, as well." Ailen squeezed Meredith's waist and let go of her. "Press the issue, lad, and ye may yet find yerself at odds. Lady Lindsey is my wife and she willna be returning to yer chieftain's house."

"Ye risk war-"

"Nay."

"Meredith," Ailen turned her toward the cabin door. "Collect yer things. We ride shortly." Meredith dragged her feet, a blatant attempt to eavesdrop. Good lord, the woman would vex a saint. Exhaling sharply, Ailen cleared his throat. Meredith shot him a quick glance and scurried inside, closing the door with a thud. He swung around and glared at the young upstart. "Dona challenge me, ye young pup. 'Tis only my wife's mercy, which keeps ye alive. Ye may return to yer home and tell Mathieus Frazer, Meredith is wed. Sinclair willna lay claim to yer clan, nor to her."

"He willna look kindly upon this insult."

"Insult?" Ailen allowed a small smirk to curl his lips. "The only insult given is the one Mathieus has offered to all within the highlands. Sinclair's loyalty to the English is enough to turn the stomach of any decent Scots."

"I will give him yer terms, but he willna accept them." The soldier whipped his horse around and thundered off.

"Mathieus is within his rights to declare war."

"Perhaps." Ailen shrugged one shoulder. "I doubt he will go to war over Meredith's marriage. Mathieus isna a fool. Sinclair isna a match for the might of our clans. Even if he wanted to attack."

"Unless they come together to get her back."

Nay, Mathieus wouldna go to war to get Meredith back. He would rely on the vague hope of convincing Ailen to let her go. That Ailen's sense of honour wouldna keep Meredith from fulfilling her duty to her father…and Sinclair. Ailen snickered, his attention on the men fading into the bush. When it came to his wife, Ailen's sense of honour was only for the woman he had claimed.

Chapter Ten

Meredith stepped from the small cottage and tugged her brat higher along her neck. The thick woolen collar offered some reprieve from the weather. A damp chill clung to the air, clouds of fog floated around her head with each exhale. Water dripped from the roof, the snow turning into slush.

The Frazer soldiers had long since faded into the highlands. They had offered little by way of protest - not that she believed they would. Young, they would stand no chance against her husband's seasoned men. Still, their departure was like a slap in the face. As if her welfare, her honor, held no more interest to her father than a bit of mutton left after a meal.

"Come, Lady Lindsey," Ailen's voice preceded his appearance at her side.

She stepped back and eyed the tall horse he sat on. Where was her own mount? If she could get her hands on her own gelding, perhaps she could ride back to her father. Attempt to explain herself and put his mind at ease. "I should return to my father, explain–"

"There is naught to explain," Ailen leaned down, wrapping an arm around her and lifting her into his lap. "Mathieus will bluster and roar for a time, but he will accept what has been done. Put yer mind to rest, wife. There will be no spilling of Frazer or Lindsey blood by either clan."

The world spun around her as Meredith gasped and grabbed his arm. Bare skin over hard muscle flexed beneath her palm. The warmth of his body soaked through the layers of fabric. The weight of his arm around her waist stirred the sparks in her blood. Her cheeks burning, she ducked her head. "Ye canna believe my father will be so easily swayed."

Ailen chuckled and tucked her head under his chin. He draped his brat around her, tightened his grip. "Mathieus Frazer is of no concern, Meredith. He is a smart man and will see the wisdom of yer marrying me."

"If ye dona worry about my father, then who… God above, ye are right? Papa is not a monster. Nay, if my clan suffers anything, it will be the wrath of the Sinclair clan."

"Nay, they willna suffer for a moment. Ye are my wife, and our arrangement goes both ways. Ye will honour yer word, as will I. If Sinclair should make any attempt against the Frazer clan, my men willna stand by."

"'Tis a tangled mess, my lord. If only it were simpler." Meredith eased herself forward, putting a small amount of distance between their bodies. Oh, if only she had thought it through a little more.

"Nay, Meredith. 'Tis not so complicated. Ye are a Lindsey and only a blempot wouldna ken how foolish it would be to attack anyone protected by our clan."

Meredith peered at him through her lashes. There was truth in his words. His reputation was one of the main reasons she had made her offer to him. But it was different. She hadna intended to marry him. Only to create enough of a stir to.

"I have put yer people at risk as much as my own." Meredith chewed on her thumbnail, a frown tugging at her brow. "Innocent blood will be spilled."

"Ye forget, if ye had married Sinclair," Ailen dropped his voice, his lips brushing against her ear. "There would have been much more innocent blood being spilled. Do ye think any of the clans would have shown mercy to a man who favors our enemy? Nay, Sinclair's fate lies within his own twisted morals."

"But–"

"Ye dona know me that well, yet, wife. So I will say this only once. Dona argues with me over war. I have more experience than ye do." Ailen nudged her with his chin. "Only God knows what the future will hold. Put thoughts of war and death from yer mind and focus on more pressing matters for ye."

"Pressing matters? What could be more pressing than war?" Meredith twisted, her nose bumping into his jaw. She eased back and stared into his gaze. "Nothing is certain, my lord, not my place within yer world. There is only uncertainty, fear, and my fate."

Ailen chuckled softly, the movement shaking her body along with his. "Yer fate is tied to mine, Meredith. I willna let anything happen to ye. Yer a brave lass, with more salt than most."

"I am a woman, Ailen. How is my bravery to help? Sinclair will be enraged. Father will bluster and storm about and caught between them–"

"Ye will focus on providing me a son." Ailen tangled his hand in her hair and pulled her head back. He winked. "A strong heir, one befitting a woman of fire and steel. That is yer only duty, Meredith. One I will do all I can to ensure is successful."

Her cheeks burning, Meredith slapped at his hand. "How typical of a man to consider only his needs at such a time. Ye willna sway my fears with talk of an heir Ailen, any more than ye will ease them with distraction."

Meredith glanced beyond his shoulder. Baird and Angus trotted among the Lindsey warriors. Baird and Angus trotted with the Lindsey warriors. There were no ropes around their wrists, no indication they were prisoners. She stiffened, the world spun around her. Nay, it couldna be. Her lower jaw worked, and she narrowed her eyes, peering at both men, yet neither looked in her direction.

"They both draw breath."

Ailen glanced over his shoulder. "Aye, they have both sworn allegiance to me and are free to decide where their loyalties dictate who they serve. It is the way of it, wife."

"But they are…" Meredith swallowed hard, her heart dropping to her stomach.

"Their explanations are theirs to give." Ailen adjusted her against his body. His hand splayed wide across her back, he held her firmly, the warmth of their combined body heat trapped beneath their brats. "Ye will have ample time to question them. To press for an explanation for their actions. They are both loyal to ye. No matter the circumstances, their loyalty canna be questioned."

"They didna stand at our wedding or even show themselves when my father's men–"

Ailen bent his head, his lips pressed roughly to hers. Short, brutal, the kiss derailed her thoughts, and she gaped at him. "Yer world has fallen into a tangled web, Meredith," he pressed his forehead against hers. "Nothing–nothing has changed. Ye are still the same woman ye were when ye approached me with yer carefully thought out ruse. Only now, ye are more and free of yer enemy."

"More? My guard has turned from me, my father is surely plotting yer demise, and Acair Sinclair is probably only now learning of the folly of his father's plan." Meredith shook her head and offered a short, harsh bark of laughter. "'Tis exhausting. All of it. This foolishness that we must survive simply to keep ourselves free."

"Then rest." Ailen shoved her against his chest and nudged his mount forward. "We have a fair ride ahead of us to return to our home. While we ride through my territory, there are always enemies lurking in the shadows. I would arrive safely."

Our home. The words sent a glacial trickle down her spine and she shivered. She was married - there wouldna be any returning to her father's home. Meredith squeezed her eyes shut and sighed. Foolish girl. So determined to do right until she stumbled into a tangled web that would see blood spilled before the first planting of the crops.

She tugged her brat up over her head, blocking out the grey light of the day, and curled against Ailen's warm chest. His warmth seeped through her clothes, the steady motion of his breathing teased her mind. Sleep - or at least the escape it offered sounded far more appealing than trying to convince her husband of how she had made a grave mistake.

Chapter Eleven

Rolling hills with snow clinging to their face surrounded the line of riders as Ailen led his men through the pass. Fresh and crisp, the breeze swirled around the line of riders, tugging gently at Meredith's hair. The scent of smoke drifted on the northern breeze as they crossed a narrow stone bridge and turned westward.

Meredith adjusted her weight in the saddle and looked upward. Flat, grey stone towered over the trail on one side, broken by the jagged cascade of ice tinted yellow. The steady dripping of water on stone spoke of warmer water beneath the surface.

A shiver drove her deeper into her brat and she rubbed her hands together in an effort to chase the chill from her skin. Her new clan's territory was cold, frozen, the kiss of spring far from its cheek.

"My lady, ye are cold?"

Meredith turned, her gaze colliding with Angus's as he trotted next to her. She clenched her jaw and focused on her horse's head. There was nothing to say to her guard. He served her husband now, not her.

"Ye are displeased." Angus's statement held a final note, an all-knowing one that grated across her nerves like a dull blade over an infected wound.

"Displeased." Meredith laughed, a cold, hard sound that offered little by way of humour. "Nay, I amna displeased, Angus. Displeased would be if I were to fall from my horse into the mud. Ye betrayed me. Ye turned yer back on everything I hold dear and swore—"

"I did what was necessary, my lady, to ensure I would be permitted to continue at yer side." Angus leaned closer, his voice dropping. "Or have ye forgotten, ye are the one who all but begged the man to wed or at least pretend to wed ye to get out of a marriage to Acair Sinclair?"

"I have forgotten nothing. My people didna deserve to suffer having that bastard as heir to the throne. My plan was sound. It would have given us freedom."

"Ye have freedom." Angus directed his horse closer. "From Acair and ye hold position within one of the most respected and feared clans within the highlands. Yer father will come to understand, just as I have."

"And Baird? What treachery did ye weave about for him? Battered, bloodied, he holds his tongue whilst ye ride about—"

"A simple family disagreement." Angus gestured over his shoulder to the man in question, who rode next to Broderick. "His cousin is married to a Lindsey soldier."

The air knocked from her lungs, Meredith twisted in the saddle to gape at the soldier behind them. Could it be? Had the clans shared a bond long before now? Did Ailen know? "Ye lie."

"Do I? Ask him yerself. Baird will confirm what I have said. Lady Meredith, ye belong to the Lindsey chieftain now. Use yer position wisely, and ye will see our people free of the Sinclair threat…and strong enough to face the English."

"At a cost ye dona have to pay."

"I canna go home," Angus shrugged. "I can only send word to my wife and children to see they come to me. Is that not enough of a payment for ye? My loyalty has not changed, my lady. I serve ye and the Frazer clan. 'Tis only possible by swearing fealty to yer husband."

Meredith glanced at Ailen and sighed. Strong willed and brutally honest, Ailen had never hurt her. He had coerced; he had prodded and teased, but he hadna forced her hand beyond what she had already committed to. As if aware of her thoughts, he peered over his shoulder at her. A slow smirk curled his lips, and he raised one eyebrow before facing forward again.

Her heart scampered in her chest, and she licked her lips. God, but he made her feel safe. Feel as though her place within his world was secure. "Ye still should have spoken to me. I understand why ye would do such a thing, but ye should have come to me. Ye couldna even come to my wedding."

"Lady Lindsey," Angus reached over and rested his hand over hers where it rested on the pommel of the saddle. "We were there. I didna feel it would be advisable to approach until after the ceremony. Ye needed a chance to get to know the man ye married."

Meredith shook her head. "Ailen isna a man who suffers fools. One only need speak to him for a moment to understand that about him. If he did, do ye think he would agree to any aspect of my plot? Nay, he put forth his own conditions and followed through." She met his gaze. "If 'tis as ye say and Baird has ties to his clan, I hold no doubt my husband wouldna prevented ye from staying by my side."

Agnus grunted and shook his head. "Ye made a right mess of the situation, Lady Meredith, and I dona think ye truly understand just yet. Baird and I are loyal to ye and Lindsey. Ye will see in time–"

"Chieftain." The rough shout drew everyone's attention to a small group of people on the other side of a narrow, cleared field. The small group crept through stumps and saplings, huddled together as if a flock of sheep cowed by a well-trained dog. As they got closer, it became clear to those approaching werena hunters or soldiers.

Nay, a woman and three small children stumbled along, an older man behind them. Blood stained their clothes, exhaustion made their steps clumsy, awkward. A gust of wind brought the weak cries of the children to her ears, the haunting sound enough to turn her stomach.

Meredith clenched the reins and nudged her mount forward. Her horse was strong, steady. The children would be safe atop him whilst they returned to Ailen's home.

"Hold," Ailen's sharp tone halted her, and she turned to glare at her husband. He met her stare, jaw clenched, lips pressed together. A muscle ticked in his temple.

"I would aid the children, husband, not finish them." Meredith bit out. Surely he couldna believe she would do anything to harm them?

"I dona question yer intent, Meredith." Ailen waved a hand, and the men thundered by her. "Only yer safety. We dona know if those responsible still stalk them."

Every muscle clenched at his words, and she gasped. It could be a ruse, a means to draw out Ailen and kill him so they could seize power without a struggle. "Who would dare do such a thing?"

"I dona know, yet. Calm yerself, wife, I know the family. They have a small farmstead at the edge of our lands and are part of our clan. Someone has set upon the family and my men will see them to us." Ailen turned away from her, his shoulders straight, one hand on the hilt of his sword. A true warlord of the highlands.

Meredith's breath caught in her throat and she choked back a sob. "Angus, ye were right. I have made a mess of everything. 'Tis my fault." Meredith wiped her face, her fingertips coming away wet. "They bear the wounds brought–"

"Nay," Baird nudged his mount closer until his knee bumped into hers. "'Tisna yer fault, Lady Meredith. Ye know as well as any of us, there are risks. Even here in the Highlands, there are those who would hurt the innocent as if they hold the right. Chieftain Lindsey is a man feared by man - those responsible will come to learn why."

Meredith nodded, Baird spoke with wisdom. Yet she couldna shake the rolling in her belly or the hot bile pressing against the back of her throat. Clenching her fists, she focused on the warriors surrounding the small group. The adults pulled the children closer, clustering together. The woman swayed on her feet, one of Ailen's warriors catching her when she crumpled. Broderick spoke, his voice hard, biting as he looked at the warriors with them. Four of them raced in the direction the small group had come.

Broderick and Ossigal lifted the children onto their mounts. The third soldier gathering the woman into his arms atop his horse. The old man shook his head and waved a hand, instead shuffling toward where the rest of the party waited.

As they neared, Meredith glanced upward. "God, grant me strength." She swung down as the soldiers galloped up. "Here, pass the children to me." Hands held out, she took the boy from Broderick and set him atop her horse. Within moments, she had all three children on her mount and was tugging her brat from her shoulders. Draping it over the children, she tucked it under them to chase away the worst of the chill.

"Chieftain," the old man wheezed as he bent double, his frame trembling like a leaf.

"Calm yerself, old man," Ailen dismounted and approached him. He stood, legs braced, hands behind his back. "When ye have caught yer breath, speak clearly of what happened."

"My lord," the woman reached out, her blood-soaked hand trembling as she wrapped her fingers around his brat. "They descended upon us with no cause. We were in the fields." Her voice broke, and a sob escaped. "We were lucky enough to escape, but the others—"

"Chieftain," the old man pushed past the warrior holding the woman, his eyes haunted. Tears clung to his lashes, and he swayed on his feet. "I recognized one of the men who descended up on us. A demon slithering about in the form of a man."

Fury and grief tangled within her chest, tightening it like a band. Why were so many so eager to harm others? Was it not enough that they faced an enemy from another country? She shook her head. Nay, there would always be those eager to snatch from others what they couldna have. If she were to guess, it was likely she knew who was responsible for this bloodshed. "Who was it?" Meredith stepped forward and caught the old man's eye. "Ye say ye recognized him."

"Aye, my lady." The old man flicked a look at Ailen, a frown tugging his brows together. "I have seen him before, a foul excuse–"

"Acair Sinclair?" Meredith raised her chin, her hand falling to the dagger at her hip. "Was it Acair?"

"Nay, Lady…"

"Lindsey." Ailen waved a hand at her, his tone brusque. "This is Lady Meredith Lindsey, my wife."

The old man's eyes widened, and his jaw dropped. He gaped at her for a moment, before one of Ailen's guards cleared his throat. The sound ripped the man from his stupor and he bowed his head. "Aye, Lady Lindsey, 'twas Sinclair, but not Acair."

Meredith lowered her gaze. Ailen's near dismissal of her stung. She was his wife. By his choice. Would all of his clan react thus? Sure their chieftain taking a bride wasna unheard of. Meredith faced Ailen, who shook his head at her.

"Nay, Meredith. Ye are not to blame for his actions." Ailen wrapped an arm around her waist and yanked her against his side. "Just as ye are not to blame for the consequence of those actions."

"And what will they be?" Meredith whispered. "What has been done is an act of war. Petty, weak. Just as the entire clan has become. I willna stand by and allow my actions to harm others."

"Ye are right." Ailen guided her to his horse and lifted her into the saddle. He swung up behind her. "'Twas an act of war. One I shall answer, the full breath of my forces, along with the men promised to me." He pulled her back against him, the hard line of his body heating her back. His thumb tucked up under the curve of one breast and she shivered. "Come. Broderick, Byran will ride with ye."

Ailen tugged his mount's head around and nudged him into a lope. He tightened his grip around Meredith's waist, his chin resting on her head. "Rest, Meredith. We are nearly home."

"How can one rest when we are on the brink of a war I hoped to prevent?" Meredith clasped her hands together.

"Ye couldna prevent the war, Meredith," Ailen's voice rumbled in her ear. "Only delay the inevitable. Sinclair's desire for the power the English would grant him blinds him to the truth. There isna a clan in the highlands that wouldna go to war with him."

"It is the innocent who—"

"Rest, Meredith. Ye worry over a man who doesna deserve yer kindness."

It wasna Sinclair she worried over - nay it was those who would fall before his men. It was the rivers of blood he would spill to avenge what he considered being his shame at her and Ailen's hands. Allowing herself the reprieve, she closed her eyes. A single tear escaped and slid down her face.

Meredith leaned back against her husband. Would his clan be so welcoming when they learned the depths of her betrayal? She had dragged them into the dark days of blood and pain. While there was nothing she could do about her decisions up to this point, by god she wouldna let more blood be spilled on her account.

Chapter Twelve

High walls of grey and brown stone greeted them as Ailen pulled up at the head of a narrow bridge. From atop the wall, Meredith caught the movement of guards. A moment later, the gates swung open with a groan and several men appeared in the opening.

Ailen moved aside and his men trotted passed them, the clatter of hooves on the bridge loud in the silence. Meredith's gelding trotted behind Angus's mount as they went by, the children clinging to each other.

"Should I send word to Papa, see if he will send forth the warriors I promised?" Meredith looked at Ailen. She picked at her nail, her heart in her throat. There was much to be done and delaying would only add to the suffering. Her father would listen to her plea of aid - and agree once he understood what she had offered to Ailen Lindsey. He had to.

"I will send word to Frazer," Ailen's words eased some of the weight from her shoulders and she exhaled a slow breath. "Along with the rest of my men. If Sinclair wishes war, I shall grant it."

Meredith tugged at a loose thread on his lien, her focus on the thin strip of leather. "I have wounded his pride, Ailen. 'Tis the only reason he would risk your wrath." Her words were soft, bitter. A tiny quiver in her tone belied her emotions. She glanced up at him through her lashes. "I dona think anyone will look kindly upon me when they learn of my part in the matter."

He lowered his gaze to her, a small smile curling his lips beneath the shadow of his beard. "Ye place too much importance on yer betrothment in his mind, Meredith. He attacked because he believes himself to have been humiliated. By a woman, no less. He thought yer father would simply hand ye over and ye would be the dutiful daughter. He was wrong and is acting out. There are too many men who believe themselves to have more worth than they possess. Put yer guilt aside, Meredith, the fault for the blood spilt doesna lay with ye."

"But–"

"Ye knew Sinclair was a bastard, else ye wouldna have approached me. Leave the war to me and my soldiers. Yer duty now is to be the lady of the clan." He captured her chin between his fingers and thumb and tilted her face up. He traced over her bottom lip, leaving a tingling trail along the flesh.

"And what duties will ye have me do? Ye canna have no expectations of me, Ailen." Soft, breathy, Meredith blinked and leaned into his touch. She licked her lips, catching the flare of heat in his gaze.

"Ye will oversee my home, Meredith, as a woman of yer position should. Ye will give me heirs. Healthy sons and spirited daughters."

Meredith chuckled. He couldna believe she would think him serious. Men wanted sons - not daughters. "As ye wish, my lord."

"My lord, chieftain," the rolling brogue of a male voice pulled them from each other's gaze and Meredith dropped her gaze to her lap. Her cheeks burning, she cleared her throat and moved so her hair fell forward, blocking the stares of those between the open gates.

Ailen nudged his mount forward, his fingers digging into her side as they rode through the gates. Meredith peeked through her hair as they rode under the catwalk. Small, sturdy cottages made of stone lined the road. Men and women gathered, staring at them as they trotted by.

Soldiers moved through the growing crowd, pressing forward to create a wall of muscle as Ailen guided his mount along the rocky path. They turned the corner and more cabins spread out like a sea of wood and stone. Smoke curled upward from the many chimneys.

Meredith blinked when Ailen pushed her hair away from her face. "These are our people. They wish to see who ye are."

A chill unrelated to the icy wind raced through her. Oh god, these were her new clan members. Men and women who were loyal to her husband - people she prayed would be loyal to her. In time. She was a stranger and they wouldna welcome her so readily.

"I can hear yer thoughts," Ailen whispered against her ear. "And ye shouldna be so focused on what is in the past. Ye are my wife, Meredith. They will be loyal to ye because they are loyal to me. Now, smile, so they can see ye are happy."

Meredith pasted a smile on her face and spoke through her gritted teeth. "Ye canna order me to be happy, husband. 'Tis not how it works."

"Ah, but 'tis how it works, because I order it." Ailen bumped her shoulder with his chin. "Yer new home, Meredith. Ye will be safe here."

But would her people?

~*~

Meredith hovered in the open door, her stomach twisting. Dust covered the surfaces of the room, hanging in the air and dancing the light from the window. Stark, empty, the room held a trunk, a massive bed, and the stone fireplace. Above the hearth two swords hung from the wall with light coloured bow nestled between them.

She stepped into the room, her fingers tangled within the fabric of her brat. Her attention settled on the bed and she swallowed. Covered in thick furs, the bed occupied most of the room. What space was left was occupied by stacks of wood and the trunk shoved against the wall beneath the window.

"Yer father will need to send along yer belongings," Ailen's voice shattered the silence, and she whirled.

"What?"

"I have sent a message to yer father, requesting yer things. Until then, I am certain we can get ye clothing. Hester will be up shortly to fit ye with new lienes. If there is anything ye need before yer things arrive, ye shall have it. Be warned, Meredith, we dona live a fancy life. My clan is far more interested in a simpler one way."

"Thank you, Ailen." Meredith offered a weak smile. "I didna have a lot of material possessions. My duty was to my clan and to the wellbeing of my people."

"Surely ye had more than one liene and brat."

"I had a few," Meredith shuffled around the room. She paused at the window and peered out. Frost clung to the glass, a thin layer of dust lining the sill. Through the frost, the distorted view of the field and lush hills spread out like a rich tapestry of green, white, and grey. "In truth, I didna spend a lot of time worrying about the collection of clothing. My people needed food, shelter, as the lady of the house. It was my duty to see to their needs. Ye forget, for a time, I had all but been forgotten about and I acted as my father's heir - until it was no longer agreeable. A daughter has but one duty to her father."

"Yer father was a man desperate for a son. 'Tis spoken of the loss of his heir and wife." Ailen cleared his throat. "Many of the clans know about yer loss."

"Momma passed from the fever, my brother shared her fate. Chieftain Frazer didna have any interest in suffering such a fate again. 'Tis one of the main reasons he didna take another wife." Meredith huffed a laugh and shrugged. She ran a finger down the pane of glass and exhaled. "I was nearly eleven summers old when Papa remembered something about me - a half-wild girl child who had grown up doing as I pleased." Meredith brushed a stray lock of hair from her face. "No matter, I am well versed in the running of a household, Ailen, so ye need not be concerned. I canna do whatever is required of me."

"Ye are very resourceful, there isna any doubt."

"What am I to do?" Meredith met Ailen's gaze. "I would know what ye expect of me as my daily duties."

"Duties. I have already told ye what ye are to do, Meredith. Ye will keep my home and provide me with an heir or two. If I am not here, Patrick or Hugh will be in charge. Should ye have any difficulties, ye can go to them."

"And ye?"

Ailen took a long and slow breath. Any hint of expression washed from his face and he looked past Meredith to the window. "What do ye mean?"

"What are ye going to do?"

"What I have always sworn to do, Meredith. There is the matter of those who attacked my clan. Justice will be served. Sinclair didna act alone. I would know who allied with him."

Ice crept through her blood, and Meredith shivered. There was little she could do to sway his mind, but she knew it wasna the Frazer clan. "And when ye find out?"

"Then they will pay for their sins. Dona stress, Meredith, only a fool would think it to be yer father." Ailen wrapped a hand around her neck, pulling her closer. His hot breath spread across her face and he stared into her gaze. "I dona have a reputation as a fool." Ailen bent his head and crushed her lips under his. As quick as the kiss started, it ended and Meredith swayed in place, her lips tingling.

Ailen turned on his heel and stomped from the room. The sound of his voice fading into silence. Meredith pressed her fingers to her lips, her gaze locked on the open door. Beneath the thin armour of flesh and bone, her heart thudded heavily. Dear god, she couldna afford to care for him.

Chapter Thirteen

Meredith wrapped her arms around herself, the retreating form of her husband and his men shrinking with each passing moment. Delivered to his home barely a day and already he rode off to confront an enemy. A warlord, like those spoken of in stories, was her husband.

"Ye need not fear he willna return." Angus appeared at her elbow. "Ailen Lindsey is nothing if not stubborn. He will return if only to vex ye."

"'Tis not his return, I fear." Meredith half turned to look at him before facing forward. "If he doesna return, who will bear the burden of blame? The outsider. I have made a mess of everything and condemned Ailen."

"I doubt he is a man easy to condemn."

"Perhaps."

"Lady Meredith, ye were aware of the risks when ye came up with yer plan. To worry yerself now–"

The man was daft. Married with children and still, he didna understand the workings of a woman's heart or mind. "It was supposed to be a simple ruse, Angus. I was prepared to accept the costs to me, not to those who are innocent. I should be home running through the day-to-day happenings of our clan. I dona belong not here, where I am an outsider. They dona know me or trust me.."

"Acceptance and trust will come in time, Lady Meredith. Ye cannot expect to climb the whole mountain in one morning."

Meredith glowered at him, turned away. Angus knew nothing of the struggle she faced. His future was set. He was a warrior who would serve Ailen. She was a woman. Her future was dependent upon her husband's generosity. If he decided it wasna worth the bother, she would be shamed and sent back to her father. If he fell, her circumstance would be far worse. Not to mention if he changed his mind, everything would all be for naught. "'Tis not the same, Angus. I had best see to my new household."

"Ye take too much upon yerself. Yer plan was sound, Lady Meredith, but ye canna control all aspects. God has a plan for us and we canna always–"

Her throat tightened. Meredith grabbed the door and yanked. "Go train with the men, Angus." The heavy door didn't budge beneath her hand. Biting back a scream, Meredith threw her weight into opening the door. "I have no desire to debate God's plan. Blood has been spilt because of a man. What more can one say? Those who suffered at Sinclair's hand need tending."

"Ye take too much upon yerself, my lady. Ye need not carry the burden alone." Angus reached around her and pulled the door open. "I will be close by."

Her head held high, Meredith walked by her guard and into the cooler interior.

She froze at the top of the stairs, heart dropping to her feet. Pressure behind her eyes preceded the first tears and Meredith swiped at her face. She was alone. There was no hope of going home. Nay, she was married and her father wouldna be forgiven for spoiling an alliance even if he didna want It.

She gathered her skirts and hurried into the foyer. Within the interior, familiar shadows danced with the flickering of candles. Meredith walked by the staircase leading upward. She paused, looking up the stone steps, and sighed. She may be hiding, but she wouldna skulk about in her room. Giving herself a quick shake, she continued on into the main hall.

At the table, the woman sat with her children. The youngest curled on her lap, dark circles beneath their eyes. Food sat upon the table, barely touched.

Meredith stumbled slightly at the top of the stairs. Finally, something she could work with. No matter the disaster, she could find a way to assist it.

"Hello, I didna get yer name when we first met."

"Oh, forgive me, my name is Edith."

"I hope we can be friends, Edith. Ye and the children look ready to sleep upon the table," Meredith clasped her hands together. "I shall prepare a room for ye so ye may rest more comfortably."

"'Tis kind of ye, lady Lindsey. We were waiting for my father."

"He is off with the men." Meredith nudged a cup closer to one of the children. I will have my guard find him. For now, come. We will get ye settled."

Silent, shoulders hunched, the exhausted family shuffled down from the table. Barely acknowledging Meredith, the weight of their scare and grief bearing down on them, they gathered at the end of the table.

Meredith rested her hand on the oldest boy's shoulder, guiding him and the others around the table and across the room. Stepping through a wide doorway, Meredith led the family down the corridor. Several servant women appeared, then retreated as quick as they appeared.

"I shall have water heated if ye would like a bath. My husband said the rooms back along the corridor are open. Perhaps a bit dusty, but still comfortable."

"Thank ye, my lady, yer kindness is appreciated."

"No thanks are needed, Edith. It is my honour to care for ye. Here, ye can have this chamber." Meredith stopped in front of a door and pushed it open. Inside was cramped, the space filled with an enormous bed. A hearth was tucked into the wall, wood stacked next to it.

It would work until she was able to secure the family a cottage. Aye, she would begin her search at first light. With a roof over their head, the family would need clothing, food. Surely there would be someone who could help gain such things for them. Who eluded her for the moment and Meredith set aside her concerns, instead focusing on the small family.

"I will inquire if anyone has clothing to fit the children. Perhaps even a toy or two." Meredith smiled at the children and stepped back.

Edith crept by, a small smile on her face. "We left so quickly I didna have a chance–"

"No explanation is necessary. 'Tis a dark day ye have survived, but we shall work together. I shall let ye rest."

Meredith pulled the door closed and retreated the way she had come. She would need to get clothing for Edith and her family. The shelter, a small cottage would do. Bedding, food, they would need so much and she would see it given. Though not as charity. If Edith was anything like the Frazer clan, her pride would be fierce.

"Ye be snooping around when there is work to be done."

Meredith froze at the harsh, bitter words. An older woman, her greying hair pulled back into a tight bun, glared at her. She held a bucket out along with a thick rag. "I dona put up with laziness. Ye will earn yer keep–"

"Who are ye?"

"Isobelle, I run the household." Isabelle studied her for a moment, her lip curling. "I dona tolerate laziness or snooping about. Ye do yer work, ye willna have a problem."

Meredith raised a brow, her gaze locked with Isobelle's. The churlish tone and disgust on her face grated across Meredith's frayed nerves. "Ah, I see, and why do ye assume I am part of yer staff?" Folding her hands in front of her, Meredith stared at the older woman.

"Dona take that tone with me, lass. Ye wouldna be the first to suffer at my–"

A bully, that was what Isobelle was. A woman given a hint of power and gone mad with it. Meredith cleared her throat and offered a small smile. Nay, she wouldna tolerate it, not when *she,* as the lady of the house. "Dona, assume ye can order everyone about Isobelle? Before you assume anything, ask. Now, there is much to be done and I havena the time to banter words." She stepped around her and continued on. The crash of the bucket behind her halted Meredith in her tracks.

She twisted around. Isobelle stood, face red, her hands clenched. "How dare ye, ye uppity tart?" She snarled through clenched teeth. "Ye will learn yer place–"

"Isobelle, ye are obviously tired. Perhaps ye should rest. Before ye say or do anything which puts ye at odds with our Chieftain…or the new lady of the house. She is not nearly as tolerant of shrews as some others." Meredith turned and stalked away, the sputtering of the maid fading into silence.

When Ailen returned, she would demand he make a formal announcement. Aye, it would put an end to such assumptions - and perhaps give her the ability to make friends. The Lindsey clan, so far, were distant and cold even compared to those in her clan.

"Dona make assumptions, either." Meredith muttered to herself. At first light, she would set to finding out the duties required by all the staff and make a plan. Aye, it was a sound plan - and one far better than the previous one.

Meredith entered the main hall and shuffled over to stand at the fire. Orange and gold flames licked along the wood within the hearth. The crackle of embers and wood burning a calming palm to her soul. Ailen would return in time.

Then she would set things to right.

Chapter Fourteen

Meredith strolled the path beyond the castle, her steps measured and level as she moved. Voices raised in song carried on the wind. Sunlight glittered off pools of water. Ice melted and created tiny rivers along the ground, cutting through the remaining traces of winter.

She shrugged deeper into her brat, the chill in her soul worse than the one hanging in the air. A heaviness sat upon her chest. One that time hadna eased with each day Ailen was gone.

It had been a week since the farm family had been attacked. Moreso, were the absence of Lindsey warriors, Ailen having taken a number and riding out almost immediately upon their return. There had been no introductions, and she was left with the challenge of a maid who considered her a servant. Isobelle would need to be dealt with, but she was loath to do it before speaking with Ailen.

Biting into the stubborn hangnail clinging to her thumb, Meredith avoided two small children racing along the road. Their laughter was a haunting reminder of what could have been lost. Stabbing pain raced along her hand and Meredith winced. A tiny spot of blood welled near the ragged nail hanging by a small piece of torn skin. She snorted a laugh at herself. Here she was a married woman and she had yet to break herself of the old childhood habit. Meredith shook her head at herself and wiped her hand off on her brat.

An older priest darted across the pathway from the small cottage he occupied in the direction of the graveyard beyond the stone walls. Several young men scurried behind him. They offered brief discussion and rarely even acknowledged her. Her eyes burning, Meredith turned away. It was yet another blow.

"He hasna returned yet?"

Meredith glanced over her shoulder at the young woman, rounded with a child standing in the doorway of a nearby cottage. The woman wore a warm smile on her face. "Nay, not yet. We have'na met yet, I'm Meredith."

"Everyone knows who ye be - or at least who Isobelle thinks ye are. Isobelle isna one ye want to run across unless ye dona mind a bit of gossip. My name is Mary, I'm Hugh's cousin."

Meredith offered a weak smile. She had seen Hugh several times, obviously he had been left behind to watch her. Did Ailen think she would flee? "He is one of Ailen's fine commanders, isna he?"

"He is. Hugh is second only to Ailen himself, and shares leadership with Patrick. Lady Meredith, standing out here willna do ye a bit of good. Come, I was just about to have a bite to eat. Join me." Mary caught her arm and directed her inside. "Our chieftain will return in time. 'Tis better they left to discover who was responsible for the attack. He isna very forgiving to our enemies."

Meredith allowed herself to be guided inside, her gaze taking in Mary's home. Cluttered but clean, the inside of the cottage was filled with warmth. Along the far wall lay the bed. Several stools flanked the table, sitting in the midst of the room before the hearth. Flames licked along the wood within, reaching up to kiss the underside of a bubbling pot.

"'Tis little doubt who is responsible." Meredith muttered under her breath. Clearing her throat, she raised her voice. "Ailen is a just man, he willna do anything without proof. Those who would dare to anger him will pay with their lives." If there was any comfort to be had, it was thus.

Deep in her heart, she knew it hadna been her clan. Her father wouldna send men to do such a dirty deed. Nay, he preferred to meet his enemy on the battlefield. There were but two options.

Sinclair - a man whose pride had been wounded by Ailen's perceived stealing of his son's bride - who she ken wouldna take pause at attacking women and children. Or, the other option–the English. A shudder ripped through her. She hadna heard of Edward's forces being so far north. Yet.

"We are at war, always at war. 'Tis a sad fact we women have learned long ago. But we are proud and strong. Our clan will win." Mary ushered Meredith to a stool and turned to the boiling pot. "Sit, sit. I dona have any wine left."

"Dona go out of yer way for me, Mary. Ye need not serve me. It is enough to have a friendly face. I would be happy to have a bit of company and talk."

"Yer very kind, Lady Meredith." Mary set a wooden bowl in front of Meredith. "Eat up, my lady. There is more than enough. War often brings hardship and we must prepare for such times."

"I pray that war will end. It is an expense no clan should bear."

"Chieftain Lindsey's men are the best trained. He would consider it an insult if they were to lose." Mary puttered around, setting a pitcher of water on the table. "God, I am certain will assure us a victory."

"Victory is welcomed. The cost to our clan isna so welcome." Meredith stirred the contents of the bowl and inhaled the rich aroma. The chill faded, replaced by warmth and the crackle of flames. She shot a quick peek at Mary, catching the other woman's paler and fine tremble in her hands. "Let us put aside such talk of war and death. It isna fit for ladies. When is yer bairn due?"

Mary rested a hand on her belly, her fingers stroking over the bump. "Soon, though, how I will raise the babe by myself I dona know."

"By yerself?"

"Aye, my man took his wound against the English last fall. He was gone when the last of the harvest was brought in." Mary's voice cracked. "It warms my heart, though, when I see ye and Chieftain Lindsey together. Such a handsome couple, and he has embraced ye."

Meredith's cheeks burned, and she ducked her head. Had she become so obvious? Married but a few weeks and already she couldna imagine not having him in her life. She wasna foolish enough to believe he loved her, nay, but he had taken her as a wife. That had to hold some weight. She took another bite, chewing slowly. He would return to her, to his clan soon, she prayed.

"My apologies, my lady. I can see I have embarrassed ye."

"Nay, I was just not aware I was so easily read." Desperate to turn on the conversation, Meredith looked around. Mary's hand moved along her belly and she inhaled. "Are there many others?" Meredith took a bite of the stew, her gaze locked on Mary.

How many of Ailen's clan were just like Mary? How many children were without parents? Surely her husband would take note of such people and ensure their well-being. Nay, it was not a duty to place upon his shoulders. It would fall to her to see the task completed.

"A few. He does what he can, but there are far greater things to worry over then–"

"Nonsense," Meredith tapped the table with her forefinger. "All the clan are important, not simply those who protect us. My husband is a busy man, one focused on protecting us from the wretched enemies who plague us. I would find a more suitable solution, aye. One that will benefit all the clan. Perhaps ye can assist me, Mary. I would know how many are in need of help within our clan. Widows, orphans, elderly members. I have already made attempts to find lodgings for Edith and her family, along with clothing, shoes, food. It would be a blessing if ye could assist me in this task."

"I will do all I can, but I dona think ye understand. Those, like myself, are often forgotten."

"I dona believe Ailen would permit such a state. Ye are valued and important and I wouldna see ye ignored." Aye, the task would give her something to focus on until Ailen returned and she could speak to him. It would be her duty.

"What do ye intend doing? We are'na treated badly, and I get meat from other families."

"I dona know yet, Mary. But I dona see Ailen allowing any of his clan to be forgotten. I will simply handle the task rather than expecting him to do so. I pray ye will help me. Perhaps we can set something up so any problems are brought to me so I may offer suggestions and if need be, I can bring my husband in to give his opinion. Together, I believe we can make this work."

Mary laughed and tugged her liene up her shoulders. "Ye are mad, my lady, but I will do what I can. Yer husband mayna be so eager."

Meredith chuckled and lifted another spoonful of stew to her lips. "He wouldna be the first stubborn man I dealt with. Nay, I will put my plan to him upon his return and get his permission."

Pounding on the door had both women jumping. Meredith shot to her feet.

"They have returned." A feminine voice called through the wood. "The men have returned."

Meredith smoothed her liene down and inhaled a deep breath. Ailen was home. He had come back to her. Stumbling over her stool, she raced to the door, throwing it open. On the other side the woman who had been knocking tripped backward.

She grabbed her arm, righting her and offered a quick smile. "Ye are certain the men return?"

"They are at the edge of the field, Lady Lindsey." She pointed toward the gates. "Chieftain Lindsey leads them. I couldna see if there were injuries."

If it was the last thing she did, she would get them to stop calling her by her title. They were her clan, her people, and didna serve her. One day soon, she would see to it. For now, the returning men must be cared for. Meredith looked toward the lower part of the stronghold.

"The men 'ave gone to war, there will be wounded."

"I pray ye are wrong. My lady, Chieftain Lindsey, will take it as a personal insult."

"Personal insult or na. It doesna matter." What if Ailen had taken a wound? The man was stubborn and wouldna show weakness to his men. Her heart dropped to her feet, and she clamped her hands together. "I didna prepare. Mary," she acknowledged the woman hovering at her side with a quick nod. "'Twas a delightful chat, but I must get back. There is much to do. Once the men are seen to, I will put forth our idea to Ailen."

"My lady–"

"Meredith," Meredith stepped out into the sun, the sound of women and children's voices raised drifting to her. "Ye may call me Meredith." There was joy in the sound and fear. Their warriors were returning. The butterflies in her belly warred with the ants under her skin. Ailen was so close.

"Ye are the wife of our clan's head, it wouldna—"

Her knuckles white, Meredith forced herself to relax her grip. How could she make them understand? "It is a greater insult to address me, as Lady Meredith every time ye speak to me. My position doesna make me above ye. My husband returns. Let us focus on their return. We will speak again. Soon." She patted Mary's arm and raced toward the stone castle.

Please dona let Ailen return, bearing a wound on my account. Bound to me as he is, he willna have it easy.

Hefting the hem of her liene over her ankles, Meredith ducked between cottages. She would need to ensure all was in readiness for his return. A growing number of clan members came out of their homes to watch their chieftain return, some blocking her path.

The small glares and harsh looks from some of the women stung, but Meredith forced them from her mind. It would take time for the clan to accept her - she was an outsider. In time, they would warm to her, she was sure of it. It was her duty to make them warm to her and one she would embrace.

Darting up the narrow steps, Meredith opened the heavy wooden door and slipped inside. She crossed the foyer and entered the main room. It was large enough to hold the returning soldiers to see to their wounds. Whilst they were cared for, she would see to it that a hot meal was prepared and ready for them to regain their strength.

"Lady Meredith?"

Meredith turned and met the gaze of one of the servants. "Aye, **Hattie.**"

"Do ye not think to be out to greet the men?"

"Aye, but there may be wounded. We must ensure they are cared for. A wound can turn sour quickly. Help me move the table, we will set the room to rights for those Ailen leads back who are in need of nursing." Meredith hurried to the table and grabbed one end. Hattie grabbed the other end. Together, grunting under the weight, they moved it from the centre of the room, closer to the fire.

Her chest burning with the need for air, Meredith leaned on the table and offered Hattie a smile. "I will go out and see how the men fare. Can ye see to a pot of hot water, bandages, and such?"

Hattie frowned. "Ye dona know yer husband well, do ye? There will be only minor injuries. If there are any."

"Many a man has fallen to a minor wound. Can ye see to it?" Meredith explained quickly. "The tiniest bit of dirt or debris can poison the wound. We shall ensure that doesna happen, Hattie."

"There is a pot of water set to boil already. And bandages have been collected and brought out. I will see to the rest of the task, my lady." Hattie whirled and vanished back the way she came.

Meredith rested her backside against the table and studied the room. Rushes were laid out across the cold stone, offering little comfort to the wounded, but they would have to suffice. It would be a challenge to get it all done without Isobelle's interference. Meredith cast an uneasy glance around the room. Isobelle either was unaware of the men's return or she was lurking in the shadows. Either way, she wasna in the room and Meredith breathed a sigh of relief.

"What in the name of God have ye done to my castle?" Ailen's voice boomed over her head and she whirled to face him. Ailen stood at the top of the steps, dirty shadows beneath his eyes, but whole.

Her heart kicked in her chest, and she swallowed around the lump in her throat. "Ye are back." Meredith pushed away from the table, her hands clenched at her sides. It was a relief to have him returned, yet beneath it was a darker note. It was as if a chasm had opened beneath her, the frustration and uncertainty broiled within her soul. How could she be so eager to see him - he was the enemy?

"Ye havana answered my question, Meredith. Ye have turned my home into…

"We made space for the wounded, Ailen. It seemed a…"

Ailen shook his head and heaved a breath before striding toward her.

"What…?"

He stopped in front of her and reached up to cup her jaw. His thumb brushed against her skin, setting it aflame with each slow caress. "The wounds such as they are, are minor, barely scratches. My men know I expect nothing less than victory, as is our reputation."

"Do still yer boasts," Meredith blinked and reached up, grabbing his wrist. Her skin burning, she licked her lips and met his stare. "Yer men may be the best Scots around, but they can fall to a blade same as any other. See them inside and I will ensure all the supplies needed are prepared."

Ailen wrapped his hand around her waist, halting her escape, and pulled her flush against him. He bowed his head, his lips caressing her ear. "I need never boast, wife."

"Ye mock me, husband." Meredith's eyes burned and she blinked against the tears threatening at the wound his mockery caused. "As if such a display isna enough to have the tongues wagging for days." Her cheeks burning, she cast a quick glance around. Open gaping from clan members preceded the rapid whispering from those in the room. Meredith ducked her head. Oh good lord, what a spectacle.

Ailen chuckled and captured her chin in his grip. He tilted her head up. "Let them wag. Ye are my wife. If I wish to kiss ye, I will do so."

Meredith sucked in a quick, shallow breath. His words shot straight through to her core. Tingles and the first tendrils of a familiar heat curled through her body. Ailen's warm breath caressed her face. Memories stirred, the need to move tugging at her limbs. She shifted from one foot to the other. Two could play at such a game. Reaching up, she wrapped her hand around his wrist and offered a small smile. "Ye have yet to kiss me. Aye, ye boast and tease. My husband is a man of action–words are for those weaker."

Ailen roared with laughter and tugged her even closer. He bent his head, his mouth settling on hers, and dominated her mouth. Meredith gasped and his tongue swept inside. Stroking, teasing along hers. A hint of ale upon his tongue seduced her senses, the warmth spreading through her body.

Tangling his fingers in her hair, Ailen tugged her head back. The movement allowed him better access, and he deepened the kiss. She bit back a whimper. God above, the man knew how to kiss. Her body on fire, Meredith swayed into him, her fingers digging into the powerful muscles in his shoulders.

Animalistic, raw, Ailen's guttural groan echoed in her beating heart. With each slow glide of his tongue against hers, Meredith's world spun. She wrapped her arms around his shoulders, arching into his body. Hot, hard, the press of his cock against her belly fanned the embers in her blood.

Meredith pulled away, her ragged breathing filling her ears. "Husband, ye make me forget myself."

Ailen squeezed her tight against his body. "Good, I would have ye think only of the pleasure we can bring to each other when ye are in my arms."

"Aye, I do." She studied each inch of his features. The faint lines of his eyes. Dark shadows lay beneath his eyes, darkening his features. Thick, dark hair covered his firm jaw. She trailed her fingers across his forehead, smearing the grim there. "Ye are weary and there are wounded to care for. I wouldna turn from the task, Ailen. I would have yer clan accept me. 'tis difficult to walk about with unease and fear dogging yer steps."

"My people will love ye," Ailen nuzzled at her temple. "In time, anything is possible. Still, now is not the time for such things. Do what ye wish. I will join my men in a swim to wash the filth from my body." He pulled away with a soft kiss to her lips. "Have the wounded brought in? Lady Meredith will see to the wounded." Half turned away, Ailen's tone hardened. "Hugh, ye will see to any of Meredith's requests."

"As ye wish, Ailen."

Chapter Fifteen

Meredith paused at the foot of the stairs, Ailen, and several men stood around the table. A small smile tugged at her lips and she turned to go into the main hall. Ailen slammed his fist on the table, his voice tight, hard, though his words were unclear.

Her husband, it seemed, was in a foul mood. Wrapping her brat around her shoulders, Meredith whirled and darted from the foyer and out the open door. She trotted down the steps. The sound of hammers and voices raised in conversation filled the morning air. Large stones encircled the marked space Meredith had asked for.

Meredith gave herself a shake and continued on the path. She sidestepped racing children and several older men in the path. A familiar cottage came into view.

"Good morn, Mary." Meredith smiled as she hurried to meet Mary by her cottage.

"Meredith." Mary offered a weak smile and ducked her head. One hand cupped the side of her belly and she braced herself against the wall with the other. "Apologies. I didna realize the hour had grown so late."

"The hour isna so late. Is it the bairn?" Rushing forward, Meredith wrapped her arm around the other woman's shoulder.

Mary shook her head and straightened. "Nay, I am fine. Ye is glowing. Enjoying having yer husband returned to ye?"

Meredith shrugged one shoulder. In the days since Ailen's return from hunting, she rarely saw him. They had exchanged only a handful of words. In truth, the only time they actually crossed paths was in the darkest part of the night when Ailen came to her bed. Conversation wasna something they worried about then.

Her cheeks heated, and she reached up, tucking a strand of hair behind her ear. "'Tis a relief to have our chieftain home."

Mary chuckled and linked her arm with Meredith's. "I can see I have embarrassed. Come, let us talk about other things. I see the men have begun building a large home near the bailey, or is it to be a meeting hall?"

"It will be a home for those who need it. Ailen gave me permission to do what I wished. I ordered it built to house not only those who dona have their own cottage, but to give us space to work."

"A communal kitchen?"

"Aye, a place to bake bread…and to weave. For now, though, it will be used as the place for those displaced by the English and our enemies until we can build them homes." Warmth filled her. There would be healing and safety.

"Ye are tiIndsey wouldna if we asked, but to even consider such a thing." Mary giggled and leaned closer. "In honesty, how many men would think of it?"

Meredith stumbled, her throat tightening. In the Frazer clan, there had been little difference to her current position. The only difference was the man behind her. A shiver raced along her spine at the thought of her husband. Here, at least, she was free to do as she pleased. Ailen had even said so. "In truth I spent much of my time running the day to day of the clan. I must admit, the notion is not my own. I learned of it from the McGreghere's wife. She did something similar, and I liked the idea."

"Mary." Sharp and brittle the tone drew both women's attention. Isobelle stomped toward them, hands clenched at her sides. Stains from the day's labour criss-crossed the front of her leine, tucked into the belt around her waist as a stout wooden spoon swayed with each step she took.

"What cause does she have to speak so harshly to ye?" Meredith stepped slightly in front of Mary.

"None that I can call to mind. In truth, she is just a bitter woman. Has been since her son married into the Frazer clan, I believe. He moved away shortly after the wedding."

Meredith clenched her jaw together. No matter what was done, Isobelle was always lurking in the shadows, ready to berate those around her. The woman was little more than a shrew. "Ye dona think she is English, do ye?"

Mary snickered. "Nay, but it leaves one to wonder."

"Mary. Ye are'na the first woman to be with child. Yet ye feel the need to shirk yer duties daily. Ye are not—"

Isobelle's poor attitude would need dealing with. Meredith resolved to catch Ailen and speak at length with him about it. For the moment, she would do what she could to prevent Isobelle from bullying her friend. "Mary is not your servant, Isobelle." Meredith stepped between the two women. Pasting a smile on her lips, she met Isobelle's gaze. "She does what she pleases so long as our Chieftain grants her permission."

"Listen yet tart, get yerself out of my way. I dona take orders from Ailen Lindsey's whore." Isobelle sneered. "When he is done with ye, he'll move onto—"

Mary gasped and clutched her chest. "How dare ye? Ye will treat Lady Meredith with the respect she deserves."

"Dona, take that tone with me."

Fury lashed at Meredith's control and she strode forward until she stood a hair's breath away from Isobelle. Staring into the other woman's face, she took a measured breath. "Ye will hold yer tongue, Isobelle, the disrespect ye have shown is enough to cause yer mother to roll over in her grave. Mary is close to her time and ye will respect that. And her position within this clan. Ye will also respect me, Isobelle. Or I will see ye cast from here."

"When Ailen is done with ye and takes my niece as his wife, ye will be the first to be removed. Ye and all of these lazy creatures." Isobelle blustered, her voice quivering.

Finally, they were to the heart of the older woman's insolence. Her own quest for power blinded her to what others saw. No matter, if Isobelle wished to remain blind, it was her flaw, not Meredith's. She was the Chieftain's wife, a lady of standing. She wouldna lose her temper. Oh nay, she would treat the situation as a proper lady.

"Meredith," Like thunder rumbling across the sky, the harsh sound of Ailen's voice drew her attention. He strode up the path, a frown tugging at his brows.

"Mind yer place, Isobelle." Meredith faced her husband, hands clasped in front of her. She clenched her hands, her nails digging into the backs of her hands.

"Ailen."

"Chieftain."

Ailen greeted the other woman with a nod. "Meredith, would ye explain to me why my soldiers have come to me?"

"How could I know their thoughts, Ailen? They dona speak to me of them."

"They voiced their concerns over yer need to build that, that monstrosity."

"Ye did say I could do what I wished." Meredith smiled sweetly. "It took the idea from McGreghere's wife. A place for women to gather to do their work while visiting seemed a suitable compromise. I have yet to see any of the women in the clan take a moment for themselves. Even their visits to each other are kept to simple pleasantries."

"Woman, the building takes space away from the training grounds. My men need to train."

Isobelle snickered behind her, and Meredith closed her eyes. Judgement or not, she wouldna be swayed. "Aye, it may. But there are advantages to having it there. Ye did say I could do what I wished." She reminded him quickly.

"I am aware of what I said." Ailen ground out. "And the building itself doesna bother me, the placement does."

"Where else should I put it? Perhaps in the field outside the wall?"

"Ye try my patience, Meredith."

"As ye do mine, Ailen. Those within the clan who have no home, or have fled the English, can find shelter–"

"Meredith, the building will remain." Ailen reached out and wrapped his hand around her arm. He tugged gently, his grim unyielding. "Its location, however, will need to be adjusted. Walk with me and we will discuss it at length."

Meredith tugged on her wrist. "Ye need not lead me, Ailen. I can walk."

"I find yer touch to be a balm." Ailen grinned at her. "I prefer to keep ye close."

Her skin tingled beneath his touch, sparks cascading along her arm. "For the love of–" Meredith fell into step with him and hid her smile. "Sweet words willna change my mind."

Ailen chuckled as he dropped her arm and wrapped his arm around her waist. He pulled her against him, and leaned toward her. "Sweet words mayna change yer mind, but perhaps 'tisna words I have in mind."

Meredith couldna stop the laughter from bubbling in her throat. "Ye left yer meeting to tease me. "'Tis day, there is no time for such foolery. Would ye not agree, husband?"

"Ye are a fine distraction." Ailen nudged her down the hill. "One I have seen very little of during the day."

"'Tisna my fault. We are both busy," Meredith cast a glance at him out of the corner of her eye. "Ye with plans for the clan, and I with—"

"Ye can lay yer plotting and planning to the side." Ailen hustled her by the men, working. "Instead, ye will speak with me. A private conversation between man and wife."

Chapter Sixteen

Driven by need, by lust, Ailen cupped Meredith's jaw. The tiny hitches in her breathing stirred the embers in his blood. He wanted. Nay, he needed her in ways he didna understand. God must have been watching over him to deliver to him a woman like Meredith.

Ailen trailed his thumb over her bottom lip, coaxing her mouth open before bending his head. Ruthless, desperate, his kiss demanded surrender. Barely leashed arousal controlled him. He pried her lips open with his, his tongue darting in to stroke along hers. He explored her mouth until he had claimed every secret.

A guttural moan escaped him when she returned his kiss. Her tongue dueled with his, thrusting and parrying. Her kiss, her touch, danced within the flames of desire.

Through the haze of lust, he shuddered when her fingers pushed his lien aside. Her nails scraped over the contours of his body, tweaking his nipples. Shudders of desire raced through him at the pain when she pinched his nipple. Her hand trailed down his sides.

Only the burning in his chest forced him back to gasp air into his oxygen starved lungs. Clumsily, his fingers plucked at the laces at the neckline of her liene, pulling the edges apart. He slid his fingers under the fabric, her delicate shiver drawing a smile.

So eager, so responsive to his touch. The only woman he had ever known who didna hide behind his expectations. The pale fabric cascaded to the floor, baring her full breasts to his gaze. Her nipples stood in hardened peaks, begging for his touch. Bending slightly at the knee, he wrapped his arms around her buttocks and lifted. Swinging her around, Ailen bore her back onto the bed, her ragged breathing echoing in his ears.

Ailen held her gaze and lowered his head. Her sharp cry of delight sent bolts of desire to his cock, his blood throbbing with the tight grip of her fingers on his shoulders. Sweet, exotic, the smell of flowers clung to her flesh. With his nose buried between her breasts, he drew a wet trail across the puckered nipple, flicking it carelessly. With each motion of his tongue, she shivered and moaned. Her hands came up to grasp his head and hold him tighter against her breasts.

"Ailen. Oh, aye. More." Her long hair drifted over her shoulders to create a curtain over his hands. He cupped the soft, yielding flesh. Pushing it together, he paid homage to the other breast.

"More? Do you want me to take them in my mouth?" he panted against her ear. "Suck them until you feel it here?" He cupped her groin, his fingers gliding through the moist curls to the swollen folds and into the slick, wet heat of her vagina. "Feel me pulling on them? Taking them deeper into my mouth until you come?"

"Aye," she whimpered, her body writhing against the tangled fabric of their bed. "Oh, please…I need you to…" She gasped when he rolled her nipple between his fingers, pulling it, then releasing it. She shuddered against him, her body arching toward him.

A ragged moan tore from his throat when she cupped his hard-on and squeezed through his lien. Meredith wrapped her fingers around his length, the soft touch of her skin scorching him.

Ailen reached up, nearly ripping his lien from his body and tossing it aside. With a groan, he grasped her hand, squeezing softly until her grip tightened around him. "Stroke me, Meredith. Oh yes, harder. Yes." He tilted his head back, guiding her movements. The slow glide of her thumb over the head of his cock drew a shocked moan. He thrust into her grasp, the moisture clinging to his cock helping to create a delicious friction.

He pulled back to meet her gaze. "You make me burn…I ache to have you. To take you hard, to make you scream my name. God above, I want to be inside you so bad…"

She smiled softly. Her eyes darkened with lust, her swollen lips parted. "'Tis as if ye read my mind, husband. The nights were too short. The days, too long. It seemed a part of me was missing." Meredith whispered, her hands clutching his shoulders. She drew her heel along his thigh, digging into his buttocks. Arching into him, Meredith whined softly and brushed her lips against his.

Each word inflamed him, the ache growing in his groin. His cock throbbed in time with his heart. He pulled her closer, his hands trapping her wrists against the bed. He bent his head.

He nipped at her breasts, marking them with minor bruises. The rasp of his tongue against the sensitive flesh drove her wild. Her hips arched against his, her legs wrapping around his hips, pulling him tighter against her. She shuddered when he moved against her, the heat from the petals of her womanhood teasing his hard cock.

Ailen loosened his grip on her wrists, dragging his hands down her arms as he explored every inch of her body with his lips. Amid her trembling explorations, she raked her fingers down his back, pulling him against her when he bent his head to suck hard on her breasts. He made love to her breasts, flicking them incessantly with his tongue, nibbling and suckling until she writhed beneath his touch.

His body shuddered at the moist throb of her loins, and he slid his finger along her folds. Her whimper of consent echoed in the movement of her body, her hips arching into his touch. He dipped a finger inside, feeling the ripple of the muscles of her vagina along his digit.

"Husband, please, no more teasing." She yanked on his hair until he stared into her eyes. "I feel like I'm about to shatter for want of you."

Ailen swallowed against the heated lust in her eyes and reached for his shaft. He rubbed the purple dome of his penis against her, spreading the clear fluid that had soaked him while he'd ravished her breasts. With a muttered oath, he shifted, bracing his legs, and shuddered at the heated glide of moisture along the dome of his erection. He met her eyes; the depths darkening to indigo with lust as he started to slide into the heated warmth.

Beneath their combined weight, the bed creaked and groaned with each thrust of his hips. His shoulders stung where her nails dug in. Meredith whimpered and arched her back. The movement drove his cock deeper into her.

The slap of skin on skin competed with the thick groans between them. Ailen braced himself on his forearms over Meredith, the pleasure swirling and building like a summer storm. Heat coiled tighter at the base of his spine, washing through like lava through to his groin. His thrusts grew clumsy until the white hot wave of pleasure crested and flowed over him.

Ailen's breath caught in his throat and he groaned, his lips pressed against Meredith's throat.

Rolling to the side, he tugged her against his chest; the sweat drying on their skin. Meredith pressed a kiss to his chest and snuggled closer. Life without her wouldna have the same joy the same passion. He needed her, not just in his bed, but in every way.

The realisation slammed into him like a runaway horse. How had it come to this? He tightened his grip on her and exhaled. He couldna tell her. Not yet. Not until their future was secured.

"Sleep, Meredith." Ailen whispered against her forehead. "I will be here when ye awake."

~*~

Boisterous voices filled the air as Meredith followed the path beyond the home she shared with Ailen, at least in spirit. Three weeks and he had yet to return. Had he truly forgotten about her or was duty keeping him from returning? Hunting the enemy seemed a paltry reason to avoid returning home.

The days seemed endless, and she often found herself pacing the floor of her chamber. The Lindsey clan hadna welcomed her. Nay, they avoided her. It made for a lonely time. Meredith gave herself a shake. The reason for his delay in return shouldna matter. She was free to do what she pleased whilst he was gone. He had offered her protection beyond her ruse and probably regretted doing so.

She shoved aside the thoughts of her husband and focused on the path. Rocky and unkept it wound through the cottages and the bailey like a wild stream. In the distance, she could make out the remaining soldiers' training. Hugh and Angus walked back and forth around the men, hands clasped behind their backs.

How her guard had found his way to training Ailen's men so quickly, she wasna certain. Perhaps by swearing his loyalty to Ailen, he had gained an equal position to what he had with her father. Meredith snickered under her breath. Mathieus Frazer wouldna be so eager to treat anyone such.

"Nay, he would have sent him as far from him as possible." Meredith shook her head and turned away. She lifted her face to the sun, a grin lifting her lips at the warmth against her skin. Finally, the bitter cold of winter seemed to be banished for a few months. The snow and ice had retreated, unveiling the rolling hills of green, trees budding and fields of color swaying in the breeze.

Casting a glance around at the cottages, Meredith tugged at her thumbnail, her stomach rolling. Simple stone cottages were lined up along narrow pathways. The doors had been thrown open to allow the fresh air into the spaces. Small patches of grass danced around the base of the walls and added the only color. Surely Ailen wouldna complain if flowers were planted about his home. It would brighten up the starkness.

She would have to take on the task and see that flowers were transplanted. Indeed, she would secure a cart and something to dig with. Each cottage wouldna need a lot, but some, and it would do her well to get in some physical labor.

"Ye are too weak." The harsh voice preceded the furious roar of a small child from beyond the pile of stones at the rear of the stronghold.

"I amna too weak. Give it back, else Pappa will hear of this."

"Ooh. Just like a baby, running and tattle on me." Laughter filled the air a moment before a furious screech ripped through the merciless cackling.

Meredith narrowed her eyes. What on earth could they be arguing over?

She gathered her skirts and adjusted her path. The remnants of a stone wall jutted out like an arm. Meredith strode around the end of the wall, a dozen boys clustered together with swords. Covered in mud, a young boy of maybe six lay at the foot of one of the older boys. Narrowed eyes and a jutted chin spoke of his rage, the tears streaking down his face revealed his lack of control.

"What goes on here?" Meredith strode forward, snatching the sword from the nearest boy's hand. Cold metal met her palm, the usual weight of the hilt familiar. She flexed her fingers around it and tucked the weapon against her side.

The boy whirled on her, lips pulled away from teeth. He reached for the weapon and she twisted away from him. "None of yer business. Ye forget yer place. Go back to yer duties and leave the men to their duties."

"Men?" Meredith stared down the upstart. "I dona see men. What nonsense has gotten into ye that ye skulk about?"

"They refuse to let us train with them." The young boy clambered to his feet. He swiped at his face, smearing tears and mud. "Pappa will hear if this William, it will be yer backside that feels the sting of his blade." He shoved William aside.

"Ye are too small. Too weak."

"I can train as easily as ye. Ye just dona want to let me."

"Enough." Meredith stepped between the two boys and looked at the small group. "How did ye come to have swords?"

"We dona have to answer to ye."

For the love of… why did males have to make things so difficult? "Do ye know who I am?" Meredith leaned closer to William.

William snickered and traced over her with his eyes. He spat at her feet and shrugged. "Just some woman our chieftain brought back. Probably a new servant to clean his house."

"William, ye shouldna speak to her like that." the younger boy glowered. "I'm Dougal, this is my brother William."

"I am Lady Meredith, Chieftain Ailen's wife." William gasped, the color draining from his face as she stared at her. Meredith smiled and tapped Dougal on the nose before she straightened. "And none of ye should be training. I dona see warriors. Not yet. A true warrior helps and teaches those weaker than them. If ye are eager to join the ranks, ye should learn to treat each other as allies. Yer brother asked ye to teach him what ye knew, William."

"Dougal is a baby."

"I am not. I just turned seven."

William glared at his brother and crossed his arms over his chest. "Yer only four."

"Seven." Dougal stomped his foot, his lower lip jutting out.

"Four."

Meredith closed her eyes and turned away to hide her grin. God, but the bickering was so very welcomed. There was something about children that could ease even the harshest burden. They would take offense to her enjoyment, she was certain. Meredith cleared her throat, drawing their attention back to her.

"Ye think ye are ready to train with a weapon?"

"Ye are a puny girl. Ye canna tell us what we are or are'na ready for." William raised his chin and crossed his arms over his chest.

A warm chuckle escaped, and Meredith shook her head. Such fire in one so young. "Let us see what ye can do." She held out the sword, hilt first. "Ye will show me."

William took the sword with both hands, a fine tremor racing along his body. Eyes wide as a trencher, he stared at the sword as if it were a wildcat he had by the tail. Aye, he was all bluster and wind.

"Chieftain Lindsey willna like it if ye hurt his girl." Dougal giggled behind his hand.

"Ailen isna here." Meredith gestured to the boys. "Show me."

The boys exchanged glances before looking back at her. She crossed her arms over her chest and raised a brow. "Ye dona wish to be warriors?"

"Yer a girl, how can ye tell us if we are doing anything wrong?"

Meredith reached out, taking the sword from William, and adjusted her grip. She flexed her fingers around the leather hilt, the weight familiar, almost comforting. She studied the blade for a moment before looking at the boys out of the corner of her eye. Balancing the hilt in the palm of her hand, she rotated the weapon. The blade sang with the movements and she braced her feet, one in front of the other. "'Tis an error you make, William. Dona judge yer enemy based on what ye can see. If ye do, ye will find yerself at the end of yer days." Meredith wrapped both hands around the hilt and swung, stopping just short of striking the boy. "I have been training with warriors since I was Dougal's age."

Straightening, Meredith rested the tip of the blade on the ground and laced her fingers together on the hilt. The boys huddled around her, eyes wide, fear and awe in their gazes. Their eagerness was refreshing, but they were not of an age to learn. She assumed it was the reason behind Ailen's refusal to accept the boys in her father's army. "If ye wish to be warriors, ye need to train. Not only to learn about yer weapon and how to use it, but to become strong enough."

"How do we do that?" Dougal pressed forward, shoving aside his brother, who glowered at him.

"Ye have all duties, tasks ye are expected to perform?"

Nods and murmurs of agreement rolled through the group as they looked at each other before focusing on her. "Aye, my lady. But we must learn–"

"Learn ye shall. The men are too busy to spend time training ye, so I will take on this duty. Ye will report to me each day before ye begin yer regular duties. We will begin with training yer bodies and minds."

A chorus of protests rose, and she silenced them with a raised hand. "Dona think it to be easy work, lads. First task ye will complete is to find yerself a solid branch, one the length of yer body. It will be yer weapon until ye are able to handle a blade. Next ye will learn to listen to instruction without arguing. A good soldier heeds the commands of his superior. Now, off with ye."

The boys scampered off, shoving and jostling with each other as they raced around the stone wall.

"Lads," Meredith turned to face them with a soft smile on her lips. "Remember, ye will be here at first light. Tardiness will be punished."

The boys nodded and raced off.

Meredith shook her head and looked down at the sword in her hands. She would need to figure out who William and Dougal's father was to see before it returned. She sighed. It would give her something to do while she waited for Ailen's return.

Sword in hand, Meredith began the walk back. She caught the looks from the other women, though none approached. Like flames licking along dry tinder, their whispers followed her through the village.

Meredith smiled. The whispers of women were irrelevant. She had a purpose, a means to connect with the clan beyond her position. The children would learn what she could teach and those in need would have a safe place to come. Aye, she had a purpose beyond being Ailen Lindsey's wife.

Chapter Seventeen

"She is giving our lord a merry chase." Baird nudged Angus and gestured to where Meredith all but ran up the hill, a sword in one hand and a bow in the other. "He maybe regretting telling her to do as she wished."

Angus chuckled and nodded. He was all too aware of Meredith's skills; he had a hand in training her. He puffed up his chest, pride racing through his body. "Aye, but it is a fine show. His regret will fade. In time."

"Ailen isna a man who does anything without first thinking it through." Patrick stomped up, arms crossed.

"Patrick, the longer ye know her, the more ye will learn. Lady Meredith isna like any other woman ye have met. She is far more infuriating." Baird chuckled and clapped the other man on the shoulder. "If she werena ye think she would have proposed such a dangerous agreement with Ailen?"

"It was a fool's game, Baird. Ye ken as well as I. Any other man would have sent her back to her father with her backside on fire." Angus scratched his jaw, his nails raking through the thick bristles of his beard.

"Meredith is the only woman who can stand her ground against Ailen. Every other woman either faints at his feet or runs screaming."

Patrick chuckled. "Angus, has she forgiven ye for yer deceit?"

Angus shot Patrick a hard look. "I didna deceive her and she will ease her displeasure in time. Not that it is any of your business." Dismissing the other man, Angus turned, surveying the open expanse beyond the wall. Sheep grazed upon the spring grass, watched by children. Soldiers mingled about. One soldier shouted something, waving a hand to the east. Those outside of the wall ran for the gate and he twisted around.

A line of riders galloped up the road. They paid no attention to those in the fields, instead they appeared to be focused only on the stronghold. Arms crossed, Angus studied the riders approaching the gates. With each stride closer to the gates, a gnawing ball of unease settled in Angus' gut and he offered a quick prayer. Damn fools.

"It took longer than I thought." Patrick and Baird appeared at his elbow. "They are Frazer men, are'na they?"

"Aye, they are some of Mathieus' most trusted commanders." Angus exhaled sharply. "Late with nary a good word to speak. Their arrival can only bring a storm and prick Meredith's temper." Angus shoved the two men aside and stalked toward the gates. "They will surely demand an audience with our Chieftain."

"Ye sound as though ye are worrying over a fight." Patrick nodded at a soldier and the man darted off. Angus eyed his retreating figure for a moment, then shrugged it aside. So long as whoever Mathieus sent minded their manners, it shouldna turn into a bloodbath.

"Worry over a fight, nay. There will be no fight. Mathieus has reached a decision. It canna be good. I wouldna have Meredith interfere until after we have heard what they have to say."

"Should we send a messenger to Ailen?" Baird glanced to the main house, his brows pulled together. The young soldier's thoughts were as clear as if he had spoken.

Angus snorted and continued on. "Let us hear what they have to say before we disturb Ailen. He was to meet with the workmen over the new house." It didna take anyone shouting at him to know Ailen wouldna appreciate being interrupted. Nay, it would be best to speak with the commanders first, then let their chieftain know.

The gates creaked open, and the riders galloped inside. Lindsey soldiers lined the road the men rode on. A silent testament to the strength of the clan and their loyalty. If God was watching, it would be unnecessary to flex their skill. Angus doubted God was looking at them.

Angus watched the familiar men ride toward them, his gaze taking in their weapons. The way they held themselves. None were eager to be within the Lindsey territory, but loyalty demanded the obedience. He met Johnas's eyes. A slight nod from the other man crushed the vague, unformed thought they were here to speak alliances. Nay, they were here for Meredith.

"We have come to speak with yer Chieftain." Johnas pulled up in front of them, the men he rode with pressing in around him, forcing the Lindsey soldiers back a step.

"Our chieftain is—"

"I bring word from Mathieus Frazer for Ailen Lindsey." Johnas's hard tone left little room for negotiation. "Fetch yer lord, so we may deliver the message."

"Johnas, Ailen Lindsey doesna take commands from anyone." Angus glanced around. The number of warriors had increased and were pressing in closer and closer. There would be no forcing Ailen into a meeting. "We are allies now. Let us discuss yer message."

"Chieftain Frazer's message is for Lindsey only."

"That is Chieftain Lindsey to ye, ye upstart." Patrick ground out, his hand falling to his sword.

Baird nudged Patrick aside, taking his place beside Angus. "Johnas, ye are a smart man. Ye know what challenging Lindsey is going to do. What word did–"

"Ailen." Angus whirled around, fists clenched. Good lord, could the day get worse? Ailen strode across the courtyard, a dark scowl on his face. Behind him, one of the Lindsey soldiers struggled to keep up.

"What is the meaning of this?" Ailen elbowed his way through the crowd. He stepped around Angus and glared at the men on horseback. "Explain this disrespect immediately."

"Chieftain Mathieus Frazer sends word." Johnas shifted in the saddle.

Ailen gestured at him, and he dismounted. Reins in hand, he approached Ailen with a stoic expression. Beneath the surface, however, Angus could recognize the coiled muscles, the tension in his friend's shoulders.

"Then give me his message." Ailen inhaled. "Walk with me, Frazer. I would know every detail of your lord's message." Johnas bowed his head and held out his reins to one of the men he had arrived with.

Angus exchanged a look with Patrick, who offered a minute shake of his head. Damn fools. A right mess of things had been made. The fault for it all could be handed to Sinclair for his greed and disloyalty. Had he not tried to bully Mathieus, Meredith wouldna have come up with such a dangerous plan.

"Angus. Hugh." Ailen barked over his shoulder as he led Johnas away from the group.

"Hugh is with Lady Meredith, sir." Angus fell into place behind Ailen. Behind him, Patrick, Baird, and several of the other Lindsey men fell into line.

Ailen whirled, a narrow-eyed glare upon his face. "Frazer, ye will tell me what message yer lord has sent."

"'Tis simple, sir." Johnas cleared his throat. "He demands Lady Meredith's return. Immediately."

"And if I refuse."

Johnas snorted and clasped his hands behind him. "I will be honest with ye, Chieftain Lindsey. My chief is no match for yer army. He clings to power by a thread, with the threat from Sinclair hanging over his shoulders at every turn. Even with the balance of power in yer hands, he is willing to go to war to get his daughter back."

"So he can barter her off to Sinclair." Ailen sneered.

Angus's blood ran cold at the notion, and he opened his mouth to protest. How dare anyone think to use her in such a manner? Did Ailen have no consideration for his wife's tender feelings? Was he? –

"The arrangement between Sinclair and my chief is complicated. I canna speak to it as I was not informed. I can assure you though, if Mathieus Frazer believes, the only way to get his daughter back and secure his clan's future is to go to war with ye–he will."

Ailen clasped his hands behind his back and strode downhill, away from the direction Meredith had taken. He released a long breath and flexed his fists. "Your lord sent ye here to tell me to return my wife to him. To surrender her to an enemy of all of Scots. A man whose loyalty is to England and Edward."

He whirled to face Johnas, his features twisted into a dark mask. A muscle throbbed in his jaw. "We are, by marriage, allies. 'Tis the only reason I dona send ye back in a box. But," sputters of protest arose around them. Ailen held up his hand, silencing everyone. "Know this. Anyone, ally or enemy, who thinks to take Lady Meredith from me will find themselves at the mercy of my sword."

Johnas shifted his weight as Ailen stepped into his space. "So, ye may go back to yer chieftain and tell him this. The only way anyone will get near my wife is over my dead body. And the cost of it will be so high the Highlands themselves will quake and burn until the ending of the world. Lady Meredith used to be a Frazer - she is now a Lindsey. She is *mine*."

Finally, a man willing to stand up for Meredith. Angus cast a quick glance upward, along with a silent prayer.

"May I speak bluntly," Johnas paused until Ailen gave a hard jerk of his head. "I canna find it within me to feel anything but relief at yer words, Lindsey. There are circumstances to which I have not been informed that make Mathieus intent on securing Meredith for Sinclair. I must respect his decision, I dona have to agree with it. War, it appears, may be the only solution."

"Indeed." Ailen grinned. "Remind yer lord his soldiers were gifted to me. All four hundred of them. Which will certainly damage his efforts."

Johnas blinked and whirled to face Angus. "Four hundred?"

"Meredith is nothing if not resourceful." Angus chuckled. "The agreement is valid."

"Indeed."

"Was there more to the message?"

"Nay, Lindsey. I shall deliver your terms to Chieftain Frazer." Johnas turned on his heel and stalked back the way they came.

Angus cleared his throat. "Johnas." He waited until the other man faced him before grinning. "Sadly for ye, those numbers include ye and yer men. Mathieus Frazer's entire army has been promised to Ailen Lindsey."

Johnas uttered a curse and threw his hands in the air. He pointed at Angus. "Ye would be wise to keep Meredith away from any talk of war, Angus. Else she may yet promise the entire Highlands to get what she desires—and leave everyone bound to everyone else."

Angus laughed as the other man walked away. He faced Ailen. "Despite the delivery of such a message, Mathieus willna challenge ye for Meredith's return."

"Then why send the message?" Patrick demanded.

"Because Sinclair is watching, and he knows he is weakened. His clan is loyal to him only so long as he is loyal to Meredith." Ailen rested one hand against his chin, his forefinger on his lips. "She is his heir, the child he forgot about when he lost his wife and son. In her he sees the future of the clan."

"Aye, Meredith isna going to agree to any terms. She has spent her entire life at the head of the clan. His grief made her old before her time and she would rather die than become Sinclair's property."

"Baird speaks the truth."

"Where did my wife go?" Ailen stared at Angus, who shifted beneath the weight of his stare. "And why would Hugh have accompanied her so readily?"

"Chieftain Lindsey," A soft voice called from behind them and they turned.

Hovering next to a lean girl, a middle-aged woman, rounded by time, with lines around her eyes, smiled. "Chieftain, I uh, I wish to say thank ye. Lady Meredith has been so kind to include the girls in her teaching. My daughter completed a successful hunt." The woman reached out toward Ailen, dropping her hand before they touched. "We just wanted to thank ye. Please, ye will thank her for us."

"Of course." Ailen nodded, and the woman and her daughter darted off, two fat hares swinging between them.

Angus side-eyed Baird and inched back as Ailen turned to face them. "Where is my wife?"

"Chieftain–"

"Angus, ye swore an oath–"

"Perhaps if ye gave yerself a moment to consider–"

"Lady Meredith is at the top of the hill. She is with some children."

Angus whirled, glaring at the young soldier half hidden by Patrick. Could the twit not keep his mouth shut?

"Angus." Ailen stomped back along the road.

"Ailen," Angus jogged to catch up, falling into step with him. "Ye did give her permission to do as she pleased."

"Aye, not to endanger–"

Angus cleared his throat and stepped in front of Ailen. Face to face with the younger man, he sighed. "Meredith wouldna endanger a child. She would fight tooth and nail for them. Her loyalty is too strong. Ye only need to consider how ye came to have her as yer wife to see the truth in my words."

"She is–"

"As wild as a winter storm. Is teaching a girl to shoot a hare a reason to punish her?"

The colour leached from Ailen's face and he bumped into Angus. "She is my wife. Mine, Angus."

"So ye are no better than Acair Sinclair? Rumour has it his first wife displeased him and he killed her. Is that yer intent? If it is, sir, I will ensure Lady Meredith is safely beyond yer reach or die trying."

"I wouldna lay a hand on her. I would kill for her, old man. I am nothing like the Sinclairs."

"Really. Ye have been married for months, and yet ye have not announced to yer clan who she is." Angus lowered his voice when he caught movement behind Ailen. "She has a tender heart and a mind as strong as steel."

"And I would protect her." Ailen grabbed the front of his lien and pulled him closer. "From anyone, including herself." Shoving Angus aside, Ailen stormed by him.

Angus followed Ailen with his gaze until he vanished around into the throng of villagers. The leashed violence in Ailen's movements spoke loudly, and he nodded. Aye, Ailen Lindsey was the only choice.

"He has no idea he is in love with her, does he?"

Angus shot Patrick a quick glance from the corner of his eye. "Nay, not yet. I think it is wise if we find something for him to focus on. Lady Meredith would be upset if the discovery was made before her warriors in training were not ready."

"Agreed."

Chapter Eighteen

Ailen pushed open the door of his home and stepped inside. Smothering a yawn, Ailen paused for a moment, his heart thundering in his chest at the silence hanging in the air. Cold, isolated, the interior of his home felt much as it had when he left to attend the clan meeting.

Where was Meredith? The days since he had gone to battle dragged on. With nearly a month between their last meeting, he was eager to see her. To touch her. His wife was an addiction he didna want to break free from.

Patrick followed closely, a silent shadow except for the way he rested his right hand on the handle of his sword. The hunt had been longer than expected and being away from home had rankled on Ailen's nerves.

"The rest of those involved will be flushed out, Ailen. Justice will be delivered." Patrick's words pulled him from his thoughts and he peered at his commander for a moment.

He didna fear Sinclair; it was those whose name had not been revealed that irked him. "Sinclair is easily dealt with. Who was he working with to attack me is the concern?" Ailen trotted down the three steps into the main hall and stomped toward the table. He poured himself a cup of water and sank into a chair. "It could be the English. He is loyal to Edward."

"Could it be Frazer?" Patrick crossed his arms over his chest. "Ye did steal–"

Ailen clenched his jaw, the muscles jumping. "I stole nothing. If Mathieus Frazer has issue, he isna a man to send someone to deal with his enemy by killing innocent women and children. Besides, he has already sent his envoy and had my conditions returned to him. Meredith is still here, within my home, and by my side."

"I dona mean Mathieus. I meant the lowlanders. Ye know as well as I, they are in bed with England. Eager to retain their lands and power under the banner of the bastard, Edward. 'Tis a bad day for the Scots when one considers the rumours of Oliphant hovering at the edge of surrender."

"Stirling Castle is a ways away, Patrick."

"Not so far when one considers it has been under siege since April."

"Even if it falls, there are those of us who will continue to fight. So long as men like Wallace and others stand against the English the fight goes on. Nay, what is happening around us has little to do with the war. It is personal."

"Could it be they heard of yer marriage? They would want the support of Sinclair as much as he wants their support."

"Nay, I have Meredith, 'tis unlikely they have the foresight to make a deal with Sinclair without her. She was the key to the entire alliance." Ailen drained his cup and leaned forward. "Nay, there is something far more –"

"A thousand apologies, sir." A middle aged woman rushed into the room. Cheeks flushed, she swayed from side to side. Her hair had escaped the braid coiled on her head. She tugged at her fingers, as if some great string threatened to rip them from her body.

Ailen bit back a curse, the woman rarely came into his presence, in fact he had seen her only twice since Meredith and he had returned. Stifling a shudder, he focused his attention on Isobelle. "What is it, Isobelle?" What in god's name could it be? Knowing her, it could be anything from someone taking issue with her scraps being tossed out to a misplaced bucket. Or to praise her niece as if Ailen would find some reason to speak to the girl.

"That…that woman, my lord." Isobelle straightened, her lips pressed into a firm, straight line. She cast a look over her shoulder before facing him with her chin raised. Scorn dripped from her voice.

Patrick rolled his eyes. "What woman? There are several hundred within the clan."

"The servant ye brought back with ye." Isobella all but cried. "She has the children moving stones. Boys and girls, sir. She's treating 'em like slaves. Such an uppity thing, why she dona talk to anybody. Refuses to do anything she is told. I told her to fetch water yesterday and she smiled at me, and continued on up the hill. Uppity. And the young ones. Chieftain, the children shouldna be pulled–"

Isobelle's insults sank like teeth into his skin. How dare anyone slander Meredith, she was kind, generous…and fiercely protective of those she cared about. Even when it got her into trouble. Slamming his palms against the arm rests of his chair, Ailen glared at his clan woman. "Lady Meredith is not my servant." Ailen rose to his feet, his words coming through clenched teeth. "She is my wife. Ye will honor her as ye honor me, Isobelle." Ailen turned from the sputtering woman. "Patrick, come, we will go find *my* wife and get an explanation from her."

"Wife? Ye married that upstart? Ye could have had any woman of–"

"Isobelle," Hard, sharp, his tone dripped with malice. "Take care what ye say about my wife, else ye will suffer the consequences. She is strong and keen. I will speak with her about her interactions with the children. Ye may go."

"Mark my words, sir, she will be the ruin of us all." Isobell huffed and darted back out the door.

"What could Lady Meredith have gotten into in the time we were gone?" Patrick fell into step with Ailen. "She doesna strike me as the type of woman who would disobey her husband."

"I do believe I know. Angus mentioned it when Frazer's were here. I didna understand what he was saying then." Ailen laughed and shook his head. How little his commander knew. *'Tis a ruse I propose, Chieftain. In exchange ye will receive a rich reward. There is –* He shook himself free of the memory and clapped the other man on the shoulder. "Ye dona know her well at all, Patrick. Meredith is the type of woman who will look ye in the eye while planning how to get what she wants."

"Ye know her better than I." Patrick capitulated.

Ailen strode up the steps and out the door. His clan acknowledged him as he headed up the pathway. "Find Baird or Angus." He commanded over his shoulder and the soldier hovering darted off.

"Ye think they would be able to tell us her mind?"

Ailen shook his head. "They are her guard. If she has gotten herself into a mess, they would be able to offer explanation." Both men had been given clear instructions, so to hear there was an issue irritated him. How many men did it take to control one woman? Although in truth, perhaps he had allowed himself to be distracted.

"You summoned me, Chieftain?" Baird jogged up, appearing from between two cottages.

Ailen turned, his attention falling to the spread of flowers in front of the building. "What in heavens…"

"They are flowers, sir." Baird grinned. "Lady Meredith insisted. She had several of us go with her and dig them up from the fields."

"Did I not say–" Ailen cut himself off and took a deep breath. "What else has she gotten into? How does it pertain to the children and carrying of rocks?"

"Lady Meredith hasna gotten into anything. She saw something in need of doing and took the duty on. If ye were wanting a lass to stay behind closed doors and wait for instruction, I fear ye have gotten yerself the wrong woman." Baird chuckled and fell into step with them.

"Where is Angus?"

"I believe he is with yer wife."

Ailen grunted and increased his pace, turning left at the fork in the path and heading for the old wall. The soft thud of footsteps behind him drew his attention. He looked over his shoulder. Gathered behind in a handful of his warriors and several women trailed after him.

The women clustered behind his men, heads bowed. They whispered amongst themselves, several nodding quietly. None of the women would meet his gaze. The sense of fear around them grating into his soul. They were aware of more than they said and feared whatever they knew would displease him. What had Meredith done?

"William, if ye are'na willing to help yer those on yer team there will be consequences." Firm, but kind, Meredith's words carried to them. Baird nudged Ailen and gestured to where the remnants of an old stone wall jutted upward.

"But my lady, they are too small–"

"William, ye willna argue. A soldier must listen to commands. Since ye dona want to help, ye will take this and three laps." Sharp, any hint of warmth was chased from Meredith's tone. "All of ye on William's team will join him."

"What is she up to?"

"William," Angus's voice cracked like a whip. "Yer lack of action affects those on yer team. For yer insolence ye will carry an extra stone. My lady?"

"Ensure they all make three laps. Elizabeth, well done. Ye are getting better with each try. Soon enough ye'll be able to help yer papa hunt fer yer supper. Being a soldier is more than simply killing on the battlefield. Ye must be able to outthink, outsmart, and outlast yer enemy. We will do one more round of practice while William and his team serve their punishment then rest."

Ailen exchanged a look with Patrick and adjusted his directly. Striding up to the stone, he rested one hand on it and peered around the corner. The space had been cleared of loose debris. Dark, rich soil had been turned up so that it covered most of the space. Along the far side, buckets sat. Angus stood, legs braced, hands behind his back staring at the gathered children.

Boys and girls of all ages were lined up facing Angus, with the exception of an older boy and five smaller children. They carried long branches across their shoulders. A small pouch with stones hung from each side of the branch, adding weight to it.

As if guided by a hand at his shoulder, Ailen stepped around the wall and took in the rest of the space. Targets had been set up along the far side of the clearing, arrows jutting out as if freshly shot.

Meredith stood, her right hand on the handle of a sword as if were little more than a walking stick. At her feet, several bundles of arrows were stacked along with numerous branches of similar lengths.

"Lady Meredith, canna we take a break?" William stumbled, dropping his load. ""Tisna fair, this doesna help us become warriors."

Meredith barely glanced at him. "Nay it doesna help ye to become a warrior when ye do nothing to learn from it. We have been training for some time, William and each day is the same. Ye spend more time complaining than ye do training. What do those who follow you say?"

"Shut up William, else we will be spending more time carrying the rocks."

"Wise counsel. Now, another round."

Angus tensed, his gaze meeting Ailen's. "Lady Meredith."

Ailen gave a short jerk of his head side to side and stepped back so while he could clearly see what was going on, he couldna be seen.

"Patrick."

"Chieftain."

"Take everyone back to their duties. I will deal with my wife." Ailen commanded. Aye, he would deal with Meredith.

"Sir," one of the women rushed forward and grabbed his arm. "Dona be too hard on her. It has been some time since I saw the joy in my son's eyes, the sense of pride he lost when his father died."

"Ye need not fear," Ailen patted her hand. "I can clearly see the benefit of Meredith's actions. Go, return to yer duties."

She bowed and scurried off after the others.

Ailen turned and leaned against the stone, his arms crossed over his chest. Aye, he would handle his wife.

"Aye, Angus. What is it?"

"Perhaps it would do to allow the younger children some rest. I am certain they will be called back to their regular duties before too long."

"Aye," Meredith stepped over the arrows and rested the sword against the wall. "Everyone is dismissed. Except for William. Tomorrow we will take a day of rest and enjoy some games. Perhaps even some treats. For now, put away yer weapons neatly and we will see ye in the morn."

"Thank ye, Lady Meredith, we will make our chief proud of us." Dougal raced up and wrapped his arms around her legs.

"Ye are welcome, now go, enjoy the remainder of the day."

The children chattered together as they put away their tools, their laughter filling the air. Once everything was hidden away, they scattered and he turned his attention back to his wife.

"William, if ye wish to be a warrior, a leader of men, ye will need to pay attention. I understand those who follow ye are smaller, weaker then ye, it is exactly why ye need to be stronger. While the others are enjoying their day away from training, ye will be here, and ye will train. Angus will guide ye tomorrow. Remember this lesson, William, not only have ye ruined yer day, but ye have interfered with Angus's as well. Now, go on."

"Lady Meredith he is eager–"

"Eager perhaps, but he looks for shortcuts. There are none in battle. Ye know this as well as I." Meredith raked a hand through her hair, ruining her braid. "Perhaps Patrick or even Hugh would be willing to speak to him. I will decide tomorrow on what to do." Meredith swung around, her gaze caught Ailen's.

He raised one brow and leaned one hip against the moss covered stone. The colour drained from her face and she swallowed audibly and stepped back.

"Angus," Ailen didna look at the man. "Ye have duties to see to."

"Ailen." Meredith protested and grabbed for Angus' arm as he walked by.

"Ye have been keeping secrets, Meredith." Ailen approached her carefully. Meredith had seen a need and taken on the duty. Baird was smarter than it seemed. He reached up, trailing the back of his fingers down her face.

"Ye have been busy."

"Not so busy I canna see what is going on. Explain why ye felt the need to teach the children–"

"They dona have weapons, save for the bow." Storm clouds gathered in her eyes and she straightened. "They need to learn, else they will hide it. I caught them playing with swords before."

"And ye didna think to give them other duties. Send them to work with the Stablemaster? Into the kitchen?"

Meredith lowered her gaze and lifted one hand to her lips. Ailen waited, a yawning pit forming in his chest the longer the silence stretched. He tugged on her arm, drawing her closer to him. "Meredith, I dona doubt yer intention. Ye know I am against—

"I could have sent them to other tasks, aye. I am aware of yer desire to prevent them from being soldiers. Experience, though, has taught me children must be children - but knowing how to defend themselves could save their lives. I was a girl when Angus caught me training. I had seen the men in the field and stolen my father's sword. Barely big enough to hold it, I am surprised I survived long enough to be caught. Within a year I had a sword of my own. I clung to it in the night when our enemy attacked. They killed women, children…those who couldna defend against them. I willna send children to war. Nor will I have them be easy slaughter." Meredith lifted her gaze to his, tears clinging to her lashes. "My father calls all boys to train from the age of twelve summers. Many see their first battle before their thirteenth."

"Teach them, Meredith, but let them be children to. I am not blind, ye have made a place for yerself here." Ailen tugged on a loose strand of hair. His heart pounding beneath his ribs, he let his gaze trail over her. A smudge of dirt crossed her nose. Her cheeks a delicate pink, freckles beginning to blossom on her skin. Sweat darkened the hair at her temple, and the neckline of her liene. "Ye are mine, Meredith, for always."

Meredith lurched forward, wrapping her arms around his waist and squeezing him. "Ye are mine as well. I willna let ye go."

Ailen brushed his thumb over her bottom lip, a smile curling his lips. Aye, he would destroy anyone who attempted to wrest her from his arms.

Chapter Nineteen

Meredith rolled over and slid a hand across the still warm material of Ailen's side of the bed. Sunlight spilled across the room, glinting off the blade laid across the trunk near the fireplace. She tossed the covers back and scooted off the bed, a giddiness racing through her. Could it be?

Kneeling by the trunk, she ran a hand along the blade. She grabbed the hilt and lifted it. Smaller than Ailen's, the weapon fit her perfectly. It wasna the one from her childhood - nay, it was long gone. Melted and reforged into a sword for a true warrior. In her hand, a gift from her husband.

Her heart fluttered in her chest and she swallowed around the lump in her throat. God, she adored him. Stubborn, gone for days, weeks, and yet Ailen had proven time and again she was worthy to him. Eyes burning, Meredith blinked and a lone tear spilled over.

She wiped at her face, drying her skin and rotated her wrist. Balanced, smooth, the blade cut through the air with a faint hum. Laughter bubbled into her chest and she pressed the hilt to her lips.

Ailen's gift was perfect. It would prove beneficial today, the children's training was coming along. Perhaps she would spar with William. Meredith set the sword on the trunk and turned, her hand outstretched for her liene. Movement beyond the glass of the window caught her eye, the light flashing off a bit of metal. She frowned and pressed closer.

Distorted figures skulked closer to the stone wall. They spilled from the edge of the trees. Weaving through the field like ants. The muted shades of their attire at odds with the lush greenery of the summer foliage.

Ice formed within her veins. Her stomach dropped to the floor. Meredith gulped in a breath, her chest tight and painful. Oh God, nay she couldna be seeing what it appeared to be. "God above is that an army?"

"Meredith?"

She whirled and gestured to the window. "They are not allies, Ailen. They rely on the fields to hide them."

Ailen strode across the room, pressing up against her. The hard line of his body warmed her as he peered out over the open field. He slammed his fist against the wall and straightened. "Blampots." He whipped-about and stalked across the room. "Fools. I willna suffer their presence."

Meredith grabbed her liene and tugged it on. She tied the lacings with shaky hands and darted after him. "Do ye think it to be Sinclair? He has already attacked yer people once." Her blood sluggish and cold in her veins, Meredith raced along the narrow corridor and down the stone steps. "'Tisna my people, of that I am certain."

"Nay, they are'na Frazer men. He is a man of some honour and would challenge me on the field of battle." Ailen braced one hand on the wall and his foot on a step. He met her gaze. "My love, yer concerns over blaming yer father must be put aside. We are allies, and while not friends, yer father and I wouldna challenge each other on the field of battle. We have something in common."

"What?" Meredith grabbed his arm. "Ailen, I know there are some who whisper about me still. My loyalty–" He pulled her closer, crushing her lips in a short, brutal kiss.

"If they speak against ye, they willna be within my clan. Ye are my wife, my heart. Ye wouldna betray me. Quickly, gather what ye will need. I would see ye to safety."

"Do ye think them to be Sinclair's forces or another enemy?"

"There are but two options for who those vermin who are skulking about are. Neither is worth assaulting yer ears." Thundering down the narrow stairs, Ailen let out a roar, his battle cry flooding the space and echoing through the stronghold.

Footsteps thundered along stone and Meredith paused midstride. Her stomach dropped and she choked back the burn of bile in her throat. She made an about-face and darted back to their chamber. Grabbing her sword, she raced back down the corridor, thundering down the steps. "Ailen, if they are–" She stumbled into the main hall.

Ailen whirled around, his face a dark mask. Gone was the loving husband, in his stead was the warlord, the Highlander preparing for war. Seeing his expression, something settled within her, the growing fear eased and she exhaled. "Ye will stay within the safety of the walls, Meredith, with the rest of the women. I willna have ye to worry about as well as those who approach."

Meredith nodded. "Of course. Those unable to fight should come within these walls. They appear sturdy and would offer–" She stepped into his path. The doors slammed open, cracking into the stone wall. Wood splintered and dust rained down on her shoulders to skitter across the worn stone. Meredith braced herself against the stone and gaped at the shadow moving across the doorway.

"Chieftain," Patrick strode through the door, a slim boy at his heels. "I have summoned all the women and children. Should we guide them to the glen?"

"Nay," Ailen lifted Meredith out of his path and stomped into the main hall. "They will remain here within the great hall."

"Ailen, it canna hold four hundred people" Patrick argued. "It could hold perhaps half that number. Where are the others to go? Or would you rather they lock themselves within their homes?"

"I would have my people safe. The path to the glen is too exposed, nay, they will go another way." Ailen kicked a rush out of the way and grabbed the metal ring attached to the floor. He tugged on it with a grunt, the creak of hinges dancing with the thunder of footsteps. Feet braced, he turned and met Meredith's stare. "Beneath our feet a series of caves flows to the North, Meredith. Ye will lead the women, the children, and old to safety there."

How on earth? Pushing aside her need to question her husband, Meredith nodded. "I dona know the way, husband. How can I lead them?"

"The path is marked. Dona argue with me, Meredith. There are enough supplies to last for several days. No matter what, ye willna return until I come for ye."

"Aye, as ye wish. We will await yer return within."

Ailen crushed her to him, his grip painful as he pressed a kiss to her temple. He slid a hand down her arm to where her fingers tightened around the hilt of her blade. "Ye are a warrior, Meredith. Ye know the risks. I will come for ye."

Amid a clamour of voices and sobbing, a wave of bodies rushed inside the castle. Twisting around, Meredith sucked in a quick breath. Women, children, the elderly, like the rushing of flood waters, they poured inside.

The young sobbed, their fear a palpable thing to her. She lurched forward from where she'd frozen, grabbing a young girl from her mother's arms. The woman's protest was waved aside as she met her tear filled eyes. "Come, we will be safe. Ailen willna let anything happen to us." She nodded toward where Ailen held the trap door. "Hurry. Yer daughter will be fine. Come, come, quickly."

Meredith shushed the little girl clinging to her. The child's fear wouldna be soothed with a few words. Nay, only the end of the battle would offer relief to their terror, victory would be their salvation. She hovered near Ailen. There were so many.

As the last of the clan members filed by her, she turned to her husband. "There are so many, Ailen"

"Aye, my clan isna small. Take care, Meredith."

Meredith licked her lips. If God was merciful the enemy at the gate was a Scots. Perhaps then they would be spared. If not, she glanced behind her where the last of the Lindsey women and children were vanishing under the trap door. "I will see them safe until yer return." She pressed a quick kiss to the babe's head and handed her to an older woman who hobbled by her and disappeared into the shadows. The fate of those entrusted to her weighed heavily upon her heart and she clenched her hands to avoid picking at her thumb nail. With a soft prayer on her lips, she leaned toward him. "If ye please, I would see sharp blades for small hands. I saw the children who have been training with me slip by, they will be protectors as easily as I." Keeping her voice low, Meredith eyed the warriors bustling through the hall.

Ailen raised a hand, his eyes narrowing. "Ye think ye can do what is necessary." Disbelief deepened his voice, a hint of mirth lay within the depths.

A slow smirk curled her lips. "If necessary, Ailen, I would cut out my beating heart to ensure the safety of those in my care. If the fate of these people is to suffer at the hands of Sinclair or the English then it is a merciful end I would offer. Dona think me weak because I am a woman. See the blades delivered and then focus upon the enemy closing in."

"Chieftain," Angus stepped into the open doorway. "The enemy will be at the gates within minutes."

Ailen gave one sharp nod of his head and waved a hand at the hovering soldiers. "Ye heard Lady Lindsey, see to it. Angus, ye will remain with my wife"

Meredith grabbed his arm, her heart skittering beneath her ribs. "Ye will take care."

"They are no match for my men." Ailen bent his head, crushing her lips beneath his in a short, brutal kiss.

Ailen stomped from the room, leaving her swaying on her feet. Her lips tingling, she pressed her fingers to them and sighed. *Please God, see him back to me, see my heart back to my chest.* Pushing the fanciful thoughts aside, she faced Patrick, who stood, a leather encased bundle in one hand. "Thank ye."

"Dona thank me, Lady Meredith. I ken why the request, dona mean I like it."

"Nay, it is a sour thought which lays heavy in my heart. But it will be the last resort. Go, my husband will need ye." She tucked the bundle beneath her arm, her fingers tightening around the sword in her hand and adjusted her liene to hide it as best she could. She wouldna look back, nay it would only make her weep. Instead, she clambered down the narrow steps, the flickering of torches casting a weak, yellowish glow to the stone.

Above her, the trap door slammed shut with a dull, deadly thud and she jumped. Her chest ached with the need for air, her rapid breathing making her lightheaded. They were trapped. No matter the consequence, there was nowhere for them to go. Meredith chewed on her nail, her gaze sweeping the gathered Lindsey clan members. Most gave her little more than a passing glance, their unease and fear nearly palpable in the air. Their safety depended upon her.

Please, God, dona let it be in vain.

Huddled in small groups, the clan members whispered amongst themselves. Meredith shuffled forward, navigating the crowd with each measured step. Fear clouded their eyes as mothers attempted to sooth the youngest children who didna ken what was happening.

Fire light flickered over the polished rock, hinting at the nooks and crannies. Among the stones, a path drifted like a lazy river. Water crashed over rock, a thunder that echoed in the cavern. The milling clan's chatter and cries did little to muffle the sound and Meredith sighed. At least there would be water. She need only to find food, blankets as if they grew out of the stone walls.

Twas a right mess, but not beyond hope. There would be time later for her panic. For now, her husband's people needed care.

"My lady." A middle aged woman stood before her, one of the boys Meredith had been training at her side. "Lady Lindsey?"

"Call me Meredith." She offered a small smile. Her stomach churning, she met the woman's gaze. "What is yer name?"

"It is a long walk to the glen. My grandson tells me ye have been training him. I have'na always been in favour of such a thing. Today I see the wisdom behind it, but I pray there is no need for him to fight."

"Momma," another woman nudged the older woman. "Patrick himself told us of our Chief's marriage. Ye dona dare to insult him by insulting his wife." She hissed, darting a peek at Meredith before lowering her gaze.

The old woman snorted and stomped off leaving the younger woman hovering in front of Meredith.

"Apologies, my lady. Momma means no insult."

"She is terrified. As we all are." Meredith breathed out and offered a weak, trembling smile. "In these trying days the enemy is vicious. I wouldna see the children to fight if we can avoid it. Put yer mind to rest for yer son's future."

"When we learned Ailen had wed a Frazer there were mixed emotions, my lady. Ye have proven our worries to be unfounded."

Her face burning Meredith nodded. "I see. And how would ye know which clan I am from? Ailen didna introduce me to anyone."

"What man thinks of such a thing. When the men returned they were talking about ye. Couldna be helped to overhear them." The woman chuckled, not unkindly and reached out to pat Meredith's wrist. "In time ye will learn, I suppose. Ailen Lindsey is a man who doesna speak his thoughts randomly. And rarely shares his plans. He is also a man driven to best his enemy. What better way for him to best Sinclair then to steal his son's bride away."

"Ailen didna steal Sinclair's bride." Meredith sucked in a quick breath. "He made a decision based on–"

"He wed a Frazer." Isobelle appeared at her elbow and Meredith forced back a sharp retort.

"Ye say Frazer as though the very name offends ye." Meredith tilted her head to the side. "Yet I have'na done anything to ye."

"Everyone knows the Frazer clan has ties to the English. There are no secrets within the Highlands."

"I rarely feel the need to explain myself to anyone, least of all a petulant shrew. Yet I shall in this instance, give ye an explanation Isobelle. My loyalty is to Scotland, to the Highlands. Any who would side with Edward and his forces are doomed to Hell. I admit some of my kin hold their position because of Edward's graces, I hold mine by my honour."

Ye would have me believe if yer former betrothed–"

"I am Ailen's wife. My duty is to him and the Lindsey clan. 'Tis not to a man I despise only slightly less than the English." Meredith smiled, the expression churning her stomach. How dare anyone challenge her loyalties when they didna know her. "Ye will hold yer tongue, Isobelle, else I will see ye from this clan. Yer intent to turn Ailen against me, to turn the entire clan against me is known."

"Ye willna last. A Frazer in a position of power, of honor– nay, ye will fall. Sooner than later."

"Perhaps." Meredith shrugged one shoulder. "If ye willna work with us, then ye are against us. Dona tempt me, I have dealt with yer kind before. For now, duty calls."

"Lady Meredith." Mary pushed by Isobelle. "What are we to do?"

"Mary, it is a relief to see ye and yer bairn." Meredith smiled at the bundle in Mary's arms. "Congratulations on a fine son. I would know if there are supplies laid in hold down here. There are many mouths to feed and keep warm. There is no telling how long the battle will rage above us."

"Ye think us to be down here so long as to need such things?"

"I learned at an early age, it is best to prepare for the worst. That way when things turn there are no shocks. The men risk their lives to save us, I wouldna have their efforts be in vain."

"And the bundle Patrick gave ye?"

Meredith paused and met Mary's stare. "A gift to set us free should the enemy prove victorious. Nothing more."

The woman stared at her through narrowed eyes. Meredith swallowed around the growing lump in her throat and waited for the other woman to speak. God had given them the challenge and they need only survive it. If the other woman doubted her, their survival would prove difficult.

"If memory serves, there is a cache of supplies within the rocks just beyond the bend. Chieftain Lindsey insisted on it being put there."

Meredith looked beyond Mary's shoulder, taking in the slight curve of the cavern. "Then we shall take stock of things and see our people fed and cared for. Come, ye will assist me. It will give us both something to do so we are'na focused on the battle."

Chapter Twenty

Feet braced apart, Ailen stared down the hill at the men slithering through the meagre foliage around his keep. It appeared to be at least a hundred men if they could be called as such. At the edge of the treeline several men sat their horses, safe from the heat of battle.

From the north a light wind carried the clank of their habergions in the stillness. Muted and distorted, the sound of the invaders' voices swirled and danced like snowflakes in a winter storm. Whoever they were, they held no fear of being discovered. Slinking from bush to bush, the weak spring sunlight glinting off their swords.

A swift look over his shoulder revealed his men dressed in their liens, swords and bows at the ready. They stood six deep, their entire focus on protecting him. Men who would crush those who approached.

"Who do ye think they are?" Baird's voice carried to him, ice dripping from the other man's tone. "Dona they know we can see them coming?"

The other man's words drew laughter from his men and Ailen exhaled. It mattered little who they were, only what they were. "Enemies of the clan. Who they are matters not. Cowards the lot of them." Teeth together, he waved Baird forward. "Ye will go with Oggisal and his warriors along the south wall. Archers to the catwalk."

"Chieftain, I am–"

"Ye are a member of my army, Baird, ye and Angus will follow orders." Ailen barked at the young upstart.

"Better with a blade then bow," Baird continued. "If ye have need of knife work then perhaps I should remain here, in the bailey."

Ailen straightened. How dare the young upstart think to instruct him. From the corner of his eye he caught movement and raised a hand. The boy would learn, if he survived long enough.

Angus shoved his way to the front and stood by Baird. He nodded at Ailen and grabbed Baird by the arm. "Better with a blade, ye may be, ye fool, ye are'na above following orders. To the wall with ye." Hissed out through clenched teeth, his words were sharp. Baird's cheeks darkened and Angus shoved him forward and followed him several steps before turning to look at Ailen. "Take care, Chieftain Lindsey, Lady Meredith will be upset if ye fall."

Ailen froze, his gaze locked on the men racing to the steps leading to the bailey walls. Aye, she would weep for his death, her heart a fragile gift he would protect. For the moment, she was safely away from the battle, but danger lurked close by. If he fell, who would be there to ease her grief? What safe harbour could she cling to?

Hugh stepped closer, nudging him. "Ye dona think them to be a risk?"

"To who?" Ailen faced his commander. Angus and Baird were loyal to Meredith and by that loyalty would serve him. Baird was kin, distant, but still kin and his loyalty had already been proven. "Baird, as ye know, is kin, and has proven himself more than once. Or do ye forget he is the one who sent word of the path my wife was travelling upon? Ye forget, Hugh. Both men are loyal to my wife, what more can I ask of them?"

"Both are loyal to yer wife. Kin or no' they are also Frazer's and—"

"They have proven their loyalty." Ailen chuckled and clapped the man on the shoulder. "One day I will explain to ye just how wrong ye are, Hugh. For now, the enemy closes in on our gates." He took a deep breath. So close he could almost hear the ragged breath as it escaped their lungs. Feel the cold steel of their swords. Aye, they were close, like flies into the spider's web.

He would make it easier for the enemy, aye. Bring them closer to their end. "Have someone loosen the barricades. Let them in so we may yet see the breath of their courage."

"It is a risk ye take."

"Nay," Ailen shook his head, there was no risk. "I have my suspicions on who lurks beyond our walls. I would see our enemies face to face. Unlock the gate. We will spring our trap here, and leave them to their fate."

Aye, they would meet their fate here, on the cold ground at Ailen's feet. He flexed his fingers around the hilt of his sword. A whistle from the wall drew his attention. From his position on the wall, a warrior gestured toward the road leading down to the gate.

Ailen nodded. Let them come.

The clatter of metal joined the thudding of rapid footsteps. Ailen shifted his weight, aware of his men pressing in behind him, his commanders at his sides. His heart slowed, a steady rhythm all too familiar. In his hand, the weight of his sword was all too familiar. Worn smooth with use, the hilt fit his palm comfortably as he lifted it as the first men rounded the bend.

They spilled over the rocky ground, pooling at the edge of the bailey. War cries ripping through the air. Light glinted off their swords and armour. The men clustered together, jeering and yelling.

A heavy pall hung over the area. Silence stretched like a thin rope.

Gravel crunching beneath his feet, Ailen roared out a battle cry and launched himself across the open space. Swinging in a wide arch, his sword whistled through the air and collided with another soldier's. Sparks flew along the screeching blades, Ailen's sword catching the other man's at the hilt. The force of the blow was bone jarring, racing along the blade and through Ailen's arms.

A snarl twisted the other man's face. "It will be yer blood on my blade, Lindsey." He ground out.

Ailen kicked his appointment back, slashing at him with his sword. Bodies clustered together. Grunts and shouts competed with the clash of swords and axes. Hot, wet, blood splattered along Ailen's bare skin.

Movement from his right caught his attention and Ailen whirled. He thrust his blade, sliding it through the middle of his attacker who dropped his axe, his eyes widened. Blood spilled from his gaping mouth and Ailen ripped his sword free.

The remainder of the attacks began to flee. His breath rasping in his chest, Ailen surveyed the open space. Soldiers covered in blood began gathering, bodies littered the ground.

Hugh shoved his way through the crowd, dragging a battered soldier behind him. The man bore more than one wound, his face marred by a deep cut. The hem of his lien was shredded, the edges stained with blood. What was left of his armour barely clung to his shoulders. A deep gash above his right eye dripped blood down his face, catching in his beard.

"Chieftain," Hugh paused before Ailen and jerked the man closer. "I assumed ye would want to have words with these blempots."

Ailen grunted and wiped the blade of his sword clean on the sleeve of his lien. He would know every detail if he had to pry it from the man's mind himself. "Indeed. I would know exactly who dares to attack my clan."

"Ye dona think I will tell ye." The man laughed, a twisted, humourless sound as he cradled his stump against his chest. "Ye arena worthy of—"

Ailen looked at Hugh and jerked his chin up. "Ye will tell me what I want to know. Do so and I will ease yer passing. Bring him." He met his commander's gaze and allowed a small smile to tug up one side of his lips. "Bring the rats as well. Patrick have some men take care of the dead so as not to shock the womenfolk." Twisting around, Ailen stomped down the road toward the lower cottages. If Sinclair thought himself capable of taking on the Lindsey's he would deal him such a blow the man would slither down to England.

"Ailen," Patrick fell into step with him. "What is to be done if these men were here to get Lady Meredith?"

Ailen's heart tripped in his chest and he clenched his fists. The metallic bite of blood hung heavy in the air along with the cries of the wounded and the dying. "He holds no claim to my wife, Patrick. Meredith is a Lindsey – and anyone who would say otherwise will suffer. If Sinclair is behind this, he will burn."

Chapter Twenty-One

Pale silvery light blanketed the ground, the moon peering through the trees. Meredith stared at it, her stomach churning. There had been no word from the men. Nothing to reveal victory or a return to their homes.

She blinked back tears, where was Ailen?

They had been clustered around the small fires near the waterfall for three days. A pall covering them like a heavy brat. Everything hinged on victory. Their entire lives hung from the dangerous edge of a sword even if they didna realize it.

"He will come?" Mary appeared at her elbow, hands cupping her elbows. "His men wouldna stand for defeat."

"'Tis not defeat that worries me," Meredith exhaled. "I worry he is unable to come. His pride willna keep him safe if the enemy presses in with too great a force. I heard that William Oliphant surrendered."

"Who is that?"

"He held Stirling Castle against Edward's forces since April." Meredith sighed and offered a weak smile. "I wish Ailen would arrive. Wish we didna have to stand guard over those sleeping."

"He will come." Mary patted her shoulder. "Come, at least try to rest."

Meredith turned, her shoulders hunched, eyes burning. She craved sleep but the haunting images of Ailen falling kept her from truly resting. A rumbling from her stomach drew Mary's attention and she shrugged. "We must take care those who need it eat. The children first." Meredith began.

A branch cracked nearby and she froze. Straightening, she reached for the sword attached to her hip. With narrowed eyes, she scanned the shadows. Her pulse thundered in her ears. A knot formed in her throat, blocking her air as she stepped back, pushing Mary behind her.

"Lady Meredith?"

"Shh." Meredith whispered, every muscle coiling with tension.

Branches rustled, and more crackling filtered through the night. Mary pressed closer, her fingers digging into Meredith's arm. "You dona think–"

"Could be the enemy. If God is with us, it will be our warriors. We must be prepared for either possibility." Meredith twisted her head to speak to Mary out of the corner of her mouth. "I will stand guard. Rouse everyone and get them prepared to move. Summon the older boys. If I fall it will be up to them to protect everyone."

"Ye canna be serious. Ailen will have yer head if he hears–"

"Go, Mary. We dona have the time." Meredith swung around. The skin around her shoulders, neck and jaw tightened painfully. Her heart threated to leap from her throat. Sweat beaded along her temple, a slow downward drag of a bead of it tickled. "For the love of God, please, Mary. Go."

Mary whirled and darted back toward the camp.

Meredith licked her dry lips, shifting her weight from foot to foot. "Please, God, if ye can hear me, grant me yer favour tonight. Send an ally and not an enemy."

The shadows moved, pressing in on her. Her knuckles ached from her grip on her sword. The meager contents of her stomach rolled in her belly and she choked back the rising burn of bile. She wouldna flee. She stood between her people and damnation.

To her right a sharp crack heralded the arrival of a moving shadow. The branches of the trees parted and a figure stepped out. Meredith bit back a cry and swung. Inky darkness swirled around them as the figure lurched forward.

An eerie whistle filled the air with each swing of her blade. Panting, her chest, aching Meredith pressed her advantage as the man stepped back. Muffled cries of a babe teased her ear and she thrust the blade, narrowly missing the man.

He darted to the side to dodge her strikes.

Behind her branches rustled. So they thought to surround her, did they? Meredith snickered. She wouldna be an easy kill. Nor would they take the children. Bracing her weight on the balls of her feet, she swung wide.

A startled gasp filled the air as the man in front of her stumbled back. She used his weakness to her advantage, finishing the movement and catching the man at her back on the tip of her blade.

"Ye will not have an easy slaughter." Meredith hissed, dragging the tip of her sword along the front of his armour.

Shadows moved through the trees pressing forward. Tears threatened and spilled over her lashes, painting her cheeks in hot trails. Nay she wouldna give up. Ailen was out there. He would come for them. He had to.

The stillness of the night was shattered by a short scream and the clatter of metal and footsteps. Terror and anger mixed in a war cry a moment before bodies raced into the night. Small, agile, they swarmed the men with whatever was at hand.

Dull thuds and pained grunts. The low curses of men and the sharp cries of boys clawed at her sense. Meredith adjusted the grip on her sword and lashed out. "We will not surrender. We willna!" The words spilled from her lips like water. Bubbling and frothing, filled with unnamed emotions as she swung again and again.

"Lady Meredith." Achingly familiar, the voice penetrated the terror clouding her senses and she whirled. Lit torches held above their heads, two men stood, Dougal in hand.

"Ye will let him go." Meredith ground out through clenched teeth. "Or I will feed yer heart to the dogs. Release him." Her blood boiling she strode forward. "I willna ask again."

"Release the boy." Deep, rough, the familiar voice sent shivers up Meredith's spine. She shoved aside the faint hint of relief and held the soldier's gaze.

The soldier let go of Dougal who sprinted the short distance to cling to Meredith's leg. "I will protect ye." He whispered. "I ain't afraid."

"Lady Meredith."

"We willna–"

"We mean no harm," The soldier stepped into the weak light, his hands clasped behind his back. "Indeed, we are honoured to be in yer presence." Meredith nearly sagged under the weight of recognition. Finally, her prayers had in some way been answered.

"Ye lie." William blustered, a heavy branch in his hand. "Ye are snakes in the grass."

"William."

"Nay, Dougal. They slink in during the night. Attacking women and their bairns. I say we send them to Hell."

"That willna be necessary." Meredith tilted her head. "Tell me, Johnas, why would ye be skulking about on Lindsey land?"

"We are allies, Lady Meredith. By yer own hand." Johnas took a step toward her, halting when William hefted his branch. "Word reached us Sinclair and some of his allies had laid siege to the Lindsey stronghold. We were honour bound to attend the battle."

"And yet ye are here in the night–"

"Aye, William. To join forces with ye until Chieftain Linsdey arrives."

"So ye have seen him?" Meredith lowered her weapon. Butterflies fluttered in her belly, please, please, let it be true. "He is coming?"

"I have'na seen him," Johnas shook his head. "Only his men. I can only assume he approaches and will reach us by mid morning. Until then, my lady, my men will stand guard so ye and yer men may rest."

Meredith looked around, her brave children surrounded them all. Weapons of every shape and size in hand. Inhaling a deep breath, she nodded. "They are well trained soldiers.The pride of Ailen Lindsey's forces. Come, we will rest. It will be a long march home tomorrow and we will need to be rested to ensure we can help those in need." She cupped Dougal's head and offered William a smile. "Back to yer bedrolls. I shall be along."

She watched the boys retreat.

"My lady, you can rest as well. No harm will come to ye."

"I will wait for my husband." Meredith waved aside Johnas' suggested quickly. So long as Ailen was out there, she wouldna rest. Not until her heart was returned to her.

~*~

A thick mist shrouded the trail as Ailen led his men toward the glen. The bitterness of knowledge settled heavy within his chest. Sinclair's men werena so loyal as to lie. Nay, they had spilled the secrets of their lord as easily as a child spilling a cup of water. He would deal with Sinclair and his allies in due time.

"Do ye think they are safe?" Angus fell into stride with him.

"I canna think otherwise." Ailen admitted. His heart clenched at the very suggestion Meredith wasna safe. When he got her back he would make certain she understood she held his heart in her hand.

"Aye, we must be close to them."

Ailen lifted his head and inhaled. The smell of woodsmoke seduced his senses and he studied the land. Dark shadows stood out through the grey-white mist. In the distance he could make out the call of birds and the faint song of a waterfall. "We are close. The glen is just around the corner. The falls mark the border and they wouldna cross it."

Ailen increased his stride, his heart thundering in his chest. They were close, so close. Once he got her back he was going to bind her to him so tightly she wouldna be able to take a step without him knowing it.

Figures appeared before them in the mist and Ailen stumbled to a halt. Every muscle tight, he grabbed his sword. Damn them all to hell.

"Chieftain Lindsey," the mist parted to reveal Johnas' familiar figure. "We have been waiting for ye."

"Bloody hell." Ailen ground out. "What are ye doing here?"

"What allies do." Johnas strode up to him, hands behind his back. "We guard yer treasures. Lady Meredith is yer wife, but she is still our Chieftain's heir. Her father would see her safe and happy."

"As would I." Ailen glared at the other man. "Doesna mean I wish to see ye every time I turn around."

"Mathieus wishes to see his daughter. Ye wish to see yer wife. Family must come before anything." Johnas cleared his throat and glanced behind Ailen before meeting his stare. "By Meredith's own hand, we are bound and I find myself eager to join the ranks of men willing to fight for her heart. I fear she is exhausted. Barely slept all night."

"Lady Meredith has always been headstrong."

Johnas chuckled. "Aye, she has. She attacked us when we arrived last night. Not a drop of blood was spilled, but between her and the boys it was an impressive defence. She is by the fire. The women finally convinced her to at least sit."

Ailen brushed by the other man and ran forward. Flickers of orange and red danced through the mist. Shadowy figures, distorted, twisted swayed too and fro, moving as if guided by an invisible hand. He darted between two trees and stumbled to a halt.

Beneath the canopy of the trees, small fires clustered together, the flames clawing at the sky. His clan gathered around them. On pikes over several fires, game sizzled. Fat hissed and popped as it hit the flames. He took in the sight quickly, his gaze landing on the woman sitting by a fire, her shoulder's hunched, a thick belt tied around her waist.

"Meredith?" The weight on his shoulders lifted when she snapped upright and twisted around to stare at him.

Meredith's lips parted, her eyes wide, she lurched to her feet. Only the quick reflexis of those sitting with her keeping her from falling. She raced toward him, tears streaming down her face.

"Ailen." Throwing herself into his arms, she clung to him. Sobs shook her entire body as she clung to him, her fingers clutching at his lien. "Ailen. Ye are here. Ye came."

"Nothing could keep me from returning to yer side." Ailen admitted pulling back to cup her face. "God above. I thought ye lost to me. Thought–"

"I didna dare to think of it." Meredith admitted. "I couldna bear to lose ye, Ailen. It has been a nightmare I couldna wake from. But ye are here, whole and safe." She burrowed against him. "Back in my arms."

"Forever." Ailen pulled her head back, his fingers tangled in her long hair. He stared down into her face. Shadows smudged the skin beneath her eyes, tears stained her pale cheeks, and yet she was the most beautiful woman he had ever seen. "I would do anything for ye, Meredith. Keeper of my heart."

"I canna lose ye," Meredith offered a teary smile. She traced over his face with trembling fingers. "But ye are safe and have come back to me. I love ye, Ailen. I didna realise–"

Laughing through her tears she wiped at her face, smearing tears and dust across her cheeks. "I know now. I willna leave ye. I know what it is my heart has always wanted. Ye are it, Ailen. God has given me ye."

Ailen grinned at her rambling and bent his head taking her mouth in a brutal, claiming kiss. Pulling back, he breathed her in. "As I love ye, Meredith Lindsey. Ye have led me a merry chase and driven me crazy but I canna imagine a world without ye in my arms."

Throwing her arms around his neck, Meredith clung to him, her tears soaking through his lien. He tightened his grip around her waist and held her. She was home, in his heart, in his arms. And he would never let her go.

Thank you for reading Married to the Enemy. It was a lot of fun to bring you these two lovers' story. If you enjoyed Meredith and Ailen's story, please leave a review on your favourite distribution site.

About the Author

Canadian Romance author, Patricia Bates lives on the Prairies with her husband and son. She's an avid reader and history buff. She writes primarily in the Historical Romance and Historical Fiction genres so if you like exciting, passionate stories set in Ancient societies, Patricia's your author.

Patricia has developed a unique writing style to reflect her passion for history and strong, independent characters. Her stories feature characters of strength and integrity, with their own unique flaws.

Other Titles by Patricia Bates

From the Shadows of Rome Series

Chains of Rome

Gladiator's Promise

Historical Romances

"The Vicomte's Prize"

"Love Thy Neighbor"

"The Preacher's Outlaw"

"Claiming her Dream"

Celtic Romances

Master's Mistress

Scottish Highlander Romance

The Highlands Kidnapped Grooms Series

"The Mistaken Groom" Book One November, 2022

"Married to the Enemy" Book Two May 2023

Abducted by the Lady – Winter 2023

Contemporary Romances

Agents of STAR Series

"Counter Strike" Book One

"Counter Engagement" Book Two

House on Grissom Road Series

"A Hunter's Desire"

"A Haunted Passion"

www.ingramcontent.com/pod-product-compliance
Lightning Source LLC
Chambersburg PA
CBHW011927050726
47591CB00009B/2377